W9-DFY-178

Clean Air and Clean Water Acts

LANDMARK LEGISLATION

Clean Air and
Clean Water Acts

Susan Dudley Gold

Marshall Cavendish
Benchmark
New York

61455

In memory of Senator Edmund S. Muskie

With thanks to Catherine McGlone, Esq., for her expert review of this manuscript.

This publication represents the opinions and views of Susan Dudley Gold based on her personal experience, knowledge, and research. The information in this book serves as a general guide only. The author and publisher have used their best efforts in preparing this book and disclaim liability rising directly and indirectly from the use and application of this book.

Other Marshall Cavendish Offices:
Marshall Cavendish International (Asia) Private Limited, 1 New Industrial Road, Singapore 536196 • Marshall Cavendish International (Thailand) Co. Ltd. 253 Asoke, 12th Flr, Sukhumvit 21 Road, Klongtoey Nua, Wattana, Bangkok 10110, Thailand • Marshall Cavendish (Malaysia) Sdn Bhd, Times Subang, Lot 46, Subang Hi-Tech Industrial Park, Batu Tiga, 40000 Shah Alam, Selangor Darul Ehsan, Malaysia
Marshall Cavendish is a trademark of Times Publishing Limited

All websites were available and accurate when this book was sent to press.

Library of Congress Cataloging-in-Publication Data
Gold, Susan Dudley.
Clean air and clean water acts / by Susan Dudley Gold.
p. cm. — (Landmark legislation)
Includes bibliographical references and index.
ISBN 978-1-60870-484-2 (Print) ISBN 978-1-60870-706-5 (eBook)
1. Pollution—Law and legislation—United States—Juvenile literature.
2. United States. Clean Air Act—Juvenile literature. 3. United States.
Federal Water Pollution Control Act Amendments of 1972—Juvenile literature.
I. Title.
KF3775.Z9G65 2012
344.7304'632--dc22
2010023503

Publisher: Michelle Bisson
Art Director: Anahid Hamparian
Series Designer: Sonia Chaghatzbanian
Photo research by Custom Communications Inc.

"Burn On" words and music by Randy Newman © 1970 (renewed) Unichappell Music Inc.
All rights reserved. Used by permission.

Cover photo: Smoke from a manufacturing plant along the Ohio River drifts upward into the air over Ohio, Pennsylvania, and West Virginia. Page 2: Foam from a paper mill in Rumford, Maine, clogs the Androscoggin River in the 1930s. A local saying described the river as "too thick to paddle, too thin to plow." Page 3: The Androscoggin River in Turner, Maine, 2007.

Cover photo: *AP Wide World Photos*: AP/Tony Dejak
The photographs in this book are used by permission and through the courtesy of:
Androscoggin Historical Society: 2; *Aurora*/Jerry and Marcy Monkman: 3, 119; *Library of Congress*: 12; LOC/Thomas J. O'Halloran, 31; LOC/Detroit Publishing Co.: 38; *National Archives and Records Administration*: 17; *Getty Images*: 85; Getty/Stephen Gorman: 6; Getty/Stan Wayman/Time Life Pictures: 28; Getty/American Stock: 49; Getty/Julian Wasser/Time Life Pictures: 65; Getty/Emory Kristof/National Geographic: 80; Getty/Alfred Eisenstaedt/Time Life Pictures: 83; *AP Wide World Photos*: AP Images: 36, 41, 43, 61 *top*, 63, 79; AP/The Plain Dealer, Joshua Gunter: 61 *bottom*; AP/Marty Lederhandler: 68; AP/Charles Tasnadi: 105; AP/U.S. Coast Guard: 114; *Lyndon B. Johnson Library*/Robert Knudsen: 54; *Corbis*/Wally McNamee: 73.

Printed in Malaysia (T)
1 3 5 6 4 2

Contents

Canoeists navigate the New Hampshire branch of the Androscoggin River. The river, once one of the dirtiest in the nation, has become a recreational destination since the passage of the Clean Water Act in 1972.

A Healthier America

U.S. Senator Edmund S. Muskie, the Maine Democrat who led the campaign to pass the Clean Air and Clean Water acts in the early 1970s, used to hold a globe in front of him, rub his finger along its shiny shell, and tell anyone who would listen that the earth's atmosphere, "no thicker than that layer of shellac," was "all that is between humankind and extinction."

The senator also saw the importance of clean water to life on the planet. He spent his childhood fishing and swimming in the mountain waters of the Androscoggin River, which flowed through his hometown of Rumford, Maine. As a youth, he witnessed the transformation of the river as its waters turned foamy and brown from pollution from the paper mill that employed most of the town's workers. Rumford became well known for air that smelled of rotten eggs and for its dirty river. Fish could not survive in a river so polluted that in 1970 the Androscoggin made *Newsweek* magazine's list of the ten dirtiest rivers in the United States.

Many others shared Muskie's passion for clean water and clean air. Who could be *for* dirty water and foul air? Yet for centuries U.S. citizens had ignored the dangers posed by pollution to the vast lands that stretched from the Atlantic to the Pacific oceans. Americans believed that the country's resources were virtually limitless. As the population grew, as people turned to the automobile as their primary mode of transportation, and as manufacturing plants took hold in cities across the nation, the effects of pollution became apparent. Sewage and garbage fouled the waters and spread disease; industrial wastes poisoned fish, clogged waterways, and filled the skies with smoke and noxious gases; and automobile exhausts blanketed cities with smog and life-threatening poisons.

Several factors delayed an all-out effort to enact antipollution laws: a general resistance to regulation, a lack of scientific and popular knowledge about the harm produced by pollution, few politicians willing to push for antipollution laws, the reluctance of states and localities to give up their own authority to the federal government, and businesses' opposition to government control and antipollution measures that would cost them money. The primary concern of the people who settled America was liberty—the personal freedom to live as they pleased. They saw early proposals to protect public health and fight pollution as interfering with their right to be left alone. Until the mid–1800s, the only health laws that won support were those aimed at fighting smallpox. Later, businesses, arguing that they should be free to run their companies as they chose, opposed pollution-control measures. While many saw pollution's effects, science had not yet progressed far enough to prove that specific pollutants caused the problems. Some pollutants—invisible gases emitted by nineteenth-century factory smokestacks, for example—would not be identified for a century or more. Typhus outbreaks, smog, oil spills, fish kills—all caught the public's attention when they occurred. Pollution became front-page news only during a crisis and then receded to the back pages when the crisis passed.

In the late 1960s a series of environmental disasters captured the public's attention and led to growing demands to clean up pollution. Compared with the sometimes violent protests over the Vietnam War, the "Save the Earth" campaign was a feel-good issue that almost everyone could back. Millions of Americans turned out to celebrate the first Earth Day in April 1970. Politicians, from town councilors to the president of the United States, recognized the popularity of the environmental movement and pledged their support.

Senator Muskie and other members of Congress who had for years been interested in environmental issues (pesticide control and conservation of land, among others) grabbed the opportunity to address the pollution problem through legislation. In doing so, they met opposition from many big corporations and state officials who considered antipollution laws to be a federal takeover. Automobile makers, coal and oil interests, shipowners, manufacturers, and steel and power companies all attempted to prevent the passage of the Clean Air and Clean Water acts. The congressional coalition, with Muskie at the helm, proceeded nevertheless.

In just three years Congress acknowledged the pollution problem, agreed that it needed to be dealt with, and enacted laws designed to correct the situation. From late 1969 to 1972, Congress passed the National Environmental Policy Act, which established the federal government as the earth's protector; the Clean Air Act; the Clean Water Act; and the

Ocean Dumping Act. During this time the federal government also banned DDT, a dangerous pesticide, and created the Environmental Protection Agency to oversee the antipollution effort nationwide.

No law by itself could rid the nation of pollution. The passage of these acts, however, represented a dramatic shift in government policy. The legislation put the federal government—rather than the states—in charge of safeguarding the nation's air and waterways. Clean air and clean water became national priorities. Congress set deadlines for polluters to reduce and eventually eliminate pollution altogether and allocated billions of dollars for sewer-treatment plants, research, and other antipollution measures. The laws relied on developing technology to enable the businesses, municipalities, and others who polluted to comply with the new regulations.

Although pollution continues to be a problem, the two acts have accomplished much in the four decades since their passage. Studies have shown that Americans live healthier lives as a result of the effort to clean the nation's air and water. Because of the Clean Air Act, pollutants that cause cancer, respiratory illnesses, and birth defects have been reduced. Lead, a potentially toxic metal that can cause serious health problems and which automobiles and refineries once released into the atmosphere, has almost disappeared from the air. The Clean Air Act forced a reduction in toxic automobile emissions—gases, particles, and other substances released into the air—even as the number of cars have increased. In addition, the act allows citizens to sue polluters when government does not enforce the law—in cases of official corruption or where agencies lack the money, expertise, or time they claim they need.

The Clean Water Act has also produced positive results. Before the act's enactment, the Cuyahoga River caught fire on a regular basis, Lake Erie had been declared dead, and the Hudson River resembled an open sewer. Today, many once-dirty rivers, lakes, and streams provide clean drinking water and places for healthy recreational activities. Since the year 2000, sports enthusiasts have lined up to participate in the New York City Triathlon, which includes a 1.5 kilometer swim along the Hudson. Canoeists enjoy the beauties of Ohio's Cuyahoga River, and fish and wildlife have returned to a much cleaner Lake Erie. Municipalities that once dumped raw sewage into the nation's rivers and streams used federal money made available through the Clean Water Act to build multimillion-dollar treatment plants. Businesses routinely include water treatment programs in their development plans.

Many advocates believe that the most important contribution of the Clean Air and Clean Water acts has been establishing the policy that all people are entitled to live in a healthful environment and that it is up to the government to protect that right. According to Leon G. Billings, a longtime Muskie aide, that viewpoint has spread around the globe.

Trash and other discarded items pollute a stream in Dubuque, Iowa, in 1940.

CHAPTER ONE

Dirty Water

At the end of the nineteenth century, the historian Frederick Jackson Turner reflected that the frontier had created the American character. Pushing ever westward, Americans learned to be practical and inventive; they used their wits to overcome obstacles and exploited every resource at hand.

Although the U.S. Census Bureau declared the frontier closed in 1890, Americans continued to cling to the characteristics that had marked their push westward. In the past they had been able to move on after depleting a region's soil and other natural resources. Eventually, however, American entrepreneurs, farmers, and business owners found themselves blocked by natural boundaries. A growing population, booming industries, and expanding farms filled once-wild lands, putting more and more pressure on the nation's natural resources. By the 1890s, when Turner proposed his frontier thesis, pollution had begun to cause problems in a number of U.S. cities.

RIVERS AS PUBLIC SEWERS

Americans first became aware of the seriousness of pollution when medical experts linked untreated sewage to disease. The first laws on sanitation were aimed at the control of smallpox. Outbreaks of cholera and yellow fever later led to the setting up of community and municipal sanitation boards. In response to epidemics of the two diseases, Congress established a national board of health in the 1870s. One of the board's duties was to find the cause of disease and develop ways to prevent its spread. The board soon discovered that America's rivers were carriers of disease.

Some experts realized early on that both clean air and clean water played a key role in the overall quality of life. "No two factors have contributed so much to the general [welfare] as the improvement of the air we breathe and the water we drink," wrote George Koker, a Georgetown University professor, in the *Journal of the American Medical Association* (*JAMA*) in 1901. Koker noted that rivers had become public sewers that carried typhoid and other deadly diseases to Americans throughout the country. He estimated that deaths from typhoid could be cut in half if residents had public sewer systems rather than outhouses or inadequate waste-disposal systems that dumped sewage into the groundwater. According to Koker, a study conducted in Washington, D.C., in 1895 showed that typhoid infected one of eighty-one dwellings without sewers compared with one of 149 homes connected to public sewer systems.

The state of Maine established the first waste-disposal plant in 1872 to serve the asylum for the mentally ill in Augusta, the state capital. Other states and communities followed Maine's lead. In the last decade of the nineteenth century, more than one hundred cities built sewage-disposal plants. These early facilities used chemicals or diluted the pollution by dumping it into larger waterways.

These and other early efforts to deal with waste often backfired. While the local community benefited from having sewage carried away by a river or stream, towns and cities downstream suffered the effects of the dirty water that flowed onto their shores. Koker contended that the water-pollution problem had to be addressed on a national level. "One of the most pressing needs is an investigation into the pollution of water-supplies when such pollution affects . . . the people of more than one state, because the individual states are powerless to protect themselves against the misdeeds of their neighbors," he wrote.

A 1906 case, *Missouri v. Illinois*, presented the U.S. Supreme Court with its first dispute over pollution affecting more than one state. The dispute arose after the city of Chicago built a $33 million, 28-mile-long canal to carry its untreated sewage into waterways that ultimately drained into the Mississippi River. The canal, among the most expensive public works projects in the nation at the time, drew fire from Missouri officials concerned that the project would pollute the river. After Chicago opened the canal in 1900, Missouri sued Illinois to stop the discharge of sewage. Missouri contended that the wastes had caused a large increase in the number of cases of typhoid in St. Louis since the canal opened. Chicago claimed the germs would not survive the trip down the river.

Although more than fifty scientists provided data for both sides during the six-year legal battle, scientific technology at the time was limited in what it could prove. Scientists had no way of testing for typhoid bacteria in the water or of proving that the Chicago sewage led to typhoid in St. Louis. In the absence of such proof, the Court ruled against Missouri. In a unanimous decision issued on February 19, 1906, the justices concluded that practically everything about Missouri's case was "involved in doubt." Justice Oliver Wendell Holmes, the author of the decision, noted, "There is nothing which can be detected by the unassisted senses—no visible increase of filth, no new smell." Missouri's case, in fact, depended "upon an inference of the unseen."

THE INDUSTRIAL REVOLUTION

Sewage was not the only substance that polluted America's natural resources and fouled its cities. With the advent of the Industrial Revolution in the 1800s, mills and manufacturing plants became major pollutants of air and water. In addition, piles of garbage and refuse overwhelmed growing cities filled with crowded tenements and factory workers' homes. In 1871 the *New York Times* reported the "horrible condition of the public thoroughfares," filled with piles of ashes three feet high, pails full of human waste and garbage, and dead animals that lay rotting in New York City streets. In other sections of the city, the reporter described gullies filled with "compost, black slime, green-hued stagnant liquids," and other filth. The "mounds of rottenness" had been in the streets for months, according to the reporter, creating "an atmosphere of death" and threatening the public health. Factories fouled the atmosphere as well, with "abominable stenches" from oil refineries, fat-boiling plants, and rendering companies that boiled animal parts to make other products. The reporter's description could have been printed about any number of other industrial cities across the nation.

Despite the terrible conditions, residents showed little interest in dealing with the situation. In the 1870s Massachusetts took an early lead in banning slaughterhouses, fat-

A man wearing a derby hat stands on a mound of oyster shells outside the C. H. Pearson & Company oyster cannery in Baltimore around 1890. Workers deposited the shells from the factory in a heap outside the grounds.

rendering plants, and soap factories from thickly populated areas. Only those that followed strict regulations could run plants near cities. But the state continued to be plagued by improper sewage disposal and air and water pollution from other sources. State legislators passed a law authorizing Massachusetts cities to set up boards of health to direct cleanup projects. But only eight of nineteen cities followed through and set up the local boards. Five cities did not even schedule a vote on the matter. "It is rare . . . that any intelligent care is given to the subject of keeping the air and water free from contamination, and excluding from streets and dwellings the deleterious effluvia that continually arise where waste and refuse matter is thrown out to take care of itself," a *New York Times* reporter noted in 1878. Meanwhile, he continued, "the people go on polluting the streams and ponds from which their water supplies are drawn with the noxious refuse of all manner of [manufacturing plants] and the reeking sewage of towns and villages, and infecting the soil and air with fumes and vapors that carry the seeds of disease and death."

In many cities, the disposal of garbage and the installation of public sewers were part of a political reward system. Officials voted for projects that improved the sections of town where they and their contributors lived, while other areas went unserved. Some politicians used their influence to delay and ultimately kill regulations that would force business owners to take often expensive antipollution measures.

In the face of public apathy and political corruption, some citizens insisted on the need for laws to protect the environment. A New York resident proposed in a letter to the editor of the *New York Times* in 1879 that a state law banning the disposal of waste into Croton Lake be extended to cover Croton River and its tributaries. "Dead cats adding flavor to the water we drink," read the letter's headline. Though meant to be sarcastic, the headline was not much of an exaggeration.

EARLY EFFORTS TO PROTECT ENVIRONMENT

Beginning in the 1870s, many cities passed laws making it illegal to dump wastes into public water sources. But many other waterways, especially large rivers, were unregulated. During that time, scientific experiments showed that water contaminated by even small amounts of waste from cholera patients could spread the disease. The Rivers and Harbors Act of 1899 became the first federal law to order controls on water pollution. The law made it illegal to dump "any refuse matter of any kind or description" into the navigable waters of the United States. Most officials interpreted that to mean solid matter; it did not include the oil and other liquids that became a major source of industrial pollution in the nation's port cities. State, local, and federal agencies for years ignored the discharge of these industrial wastes into the rivers.

By the 1920s several major cities faced serious pollution problems that threatened fisheries, tourism, and the health of local residents. In February 1921 the Army Corps of Engineers reported that New York City sewers were discharging "large quantities of oil" into the harbor. Tankers and refineries also contributed to the oily mess that polluted New York and several other harbor cities. A fire had already raged through the docks of New Orleans after a hot metal bolt fell into the harbor and set the oily waters there ablaze. Harbors in Mobile, Alabama, and Baltimore had also been damaged by fires originating from oil discharges.

States began calling for federal action to address the problem. In June 1921 Representative T. Frank Appleby of New Jersey introduced the Oil Pollution Act, which made it a federal offense to dump oil in navigable waters. Under the bill, violators would face a fine of $2,500 for each offense. New Jersey Senator Joseph S. Frelinghuysen presented an identical bill in the Senate. According to Appleby, the tonnage of oil-burning vessels sailing into U.S. ports had jumped from 5 million in 1919 to 19 million in 1921, with a corresponding rise in pollution. Much of the harbor pollution came from foreign ships that dumped oil and wastes outside the three-mile limit, where U.S. laws did not apply. Ships often let seawater into their oil tanks for ballast and discharged the contaminated water before reloading.

Congressional hearings on the bill began in January 1922, with coastal states lining up in favor. New York and New Jersey officials testified that coastal pollution had "increased the fire hazards, made bathing at many beaches unsanitary, depreciated the value of seashore property and killed huge quantities of fish." The oil deposits also threatened several species of migratory birds. Water contamination, which extended "for many miles out to sea," was caused in part by ships and manufacturing plants that threw out "increasing quantities of tar and oil wastes." The National Coast Anti-Pollution League, a coalition of state and local officials in the Atlantic states, urged Congress to pass the bill. The group's national convention, held August 10–11, 1922, attracted widespread attention to the antipollution cause. Representatives from trade organizations and chambers of commerce, who regarded pollution as a threat to their region's economy, joined local and state officials at the convention.

The Senate approved the Oil Pollution Act in early 1923, but the House defeated the measure before adjourning in March. The biggest stumbling block came from opposition from onshore manufacturers, who refused to support the bill unless it excluded their plants. As proposed, the bill barred ships and land-based plants from dumping oil and other wastes into coastal waters. In November 1923 Frelinghuysen, who had ushered the bill through the Senate but had failed to win reelection, called a meeting of proponents and opponents to try to work out a compromise. The effort failed, and a faction of the National Coast Anti-Pollution League joined the manufacturers in weakening the bill. The law passed by Congress in 1924 excluded land-based plants from the dumping ban and set fines of $50 to $2,500 or jail sentences of up to one year for violators.

In a report prepared for Congress on ways to deal with oil pollution, the Bureau of Mines recommended that the government limit waste disposal by manufacturing plants sited along the shore, require ships to install devices to prevent petroleum wastes from being dumped along with discarded water, and promote the use of barges to collect waste oil from ships at sea. These were among the topics discussed when the International Conference on Oil Pollution, convened by President Calvin Coolidge, assembled in Washington on June 8, 1926. Twelve nations—including most coastal European countries, Japan, and the United States—sent delegates to the assembly. Nearly all maritime countries had by then passed laws regulating pollution along their own shores.

The problem required international efforts, however, to control discharges at sea that affected adjacent lands. Delegates eventually voted to ban the discharge of oil in waters within fifty to 150 miles of the shore. Despite the agreement, the quality of water along the Atlantic coast of the United States continued to worsen. A passage from New York's Regional Plan—one of the first to address such issues as controlling land use and preserving natural resources—cited one reason: "Government regulation alone cannot remedy conditions unless public sentiment is ready to demand a strict enforcement of the necessary laws."

In 1936 Senator Augustine Lonergan, a Connecticut Democrat, introduced a bill to set up regional watershed sanitary districts to control the discharge of untreated waste into the nation's waterways. Many businesses opposed the legislation. They argued that states should control the waterways within their borders, that there were enough antipollution laws on the books, that industrial water pollution was unavoidable, and that measures to clean up rivers and streams would be too expensive and would result in a loss of jobs. Congress failed to act on the bill or on others that addressed the wastewater issue before adjourning in June.

During the next session, the new Congress enacted a weaker antipollution bill. Agreeing with business interests opposed to the bill, the House and the Senate eliminated several aspects of the original measure: watershed districts, purity and treatment standards for water, and federal enforcement of the act's provisions. The Water Pollution Control Act did, however, call for the creation of a Division of Water Pollution Control within the Public Health Service and directed state, federal, and local agencies to prepare plans to eliminate or reduce water pollution in navigable waters in the United States.

It also withheld federal grants for treatment plants from states and municipalities that dumped untreated waste and sewage into the nation's waterways. Congress set aside $1 million to run the new division and to aid state health authorities. Conservationists opposed the bill and urged President Franklin D. Roosevelt to veto it. Roosevelt went along with their wishes, but he said he vetoed the bill because it gave Congress the authority to control funding requests for pollution-control projects.

In March 1940 the House passed a revised bill that set up a separate department within the Public Health Service to deal with water pollution and also allocated $250,000 to administer the law. The House version required all industries operating near streams and other waterways to obtain federal permits. It also ended federal grants and replaced them with loans to states seeking funds for antipollution projects. Several controversial amendments, however, doomed the bill in the Senate. After December 1941, when the Japanese attack on Pearl Harbor brought the United States into World War II, Congress's focus became the war and related issues. It did not address water pollution again until peacetime.

THE FIRST WATER POLLUTION CONTROL ACT

Water-pollution problems continued to plague American cities and towns throughout the 1940s. Typhoid fever and hundreds of cases of intestinal disorders struck residents in Rochester, New York, in December 1940, after untreated sewage accidentally poured into the Genesee River, which provided drinking water for the city. In other incidents, pollution forced the temporary closing of beaches all along the Atlantic seaboard and threatened the health of swimmers. By war's end, reports on dangerously polluted water began to appear regularly in the nation's newspapers. In January 1947 the chief geologist of the Kansas State Board of Health warned that the nation faced water rationing if the United States did not take action to curb pollution. The problem, he said, also threatened the country's economic growth and industrial expansion. Contrary to the popular belief that the water supply was "inexhaustible," the scientist reported that 75 percent of the springs and wells in the eastern states had ceased to provide drinking water in the past fifty years. He and others called for conservation and antipollution measures.

Surgeon General Thomas Parran took the lead in urging Congress to deal with water pollution. The "gross pollution" of America's rivers and streams that provided the nation's drinking water threatened the national health and welfare, Parran told a gathering of the American Chemical Society in April 1947. He proposed the establishment of a federal agency to oversee state water-treatment programs and with authority to enforce antipollution measures.

The Senate passed the Water Pollution Control Act on July 16, 1947, a law that attempted to address many of Parran's concerns. After months of delay, the House voted overwhelmingly, 138 to 14, for a similar bill. The final version called for $24.5 million in loans and grants for state and local water-pollution-control projects, established a national research center on the issue, and stipulated that those who polluted the nation's rivers and streams could be sued in federal courts. On June 30, 1948, President Harry S. Truman signed the bill, the first to make water pollution a federal concern. Later that year the federal government set up fourteen regional offices to oversee water-pollution-control efforts throughout the country. The federal government never funded the loan program, however, and states had to pay for pollution-control projects on their own.

Efforts among states produced some good results. In August 1950 the *New York Times* reported that pollution in the ocean and river waters of New York, New Jersey, and Connecticut had been cut in half in the preceding thirteen years. According to the report, the three states had spent $150 million to treat 800 million gallons of sewage discharged each day into the region's waters (another 800 million gallons of sewage still flowed into the waters untreated). Officials estimated it would take another nine years and almost $300 million to clean up the entire sewage outflow.

Industrial wastes continued to contribute to the nation's water pollution problems. Thousands of fish died after liquid cyanide from a closed electroplating plant leached into the Mettowee River in Albany, New York, in May 1950. Other cities reported damages caused by oil spills, heavy metals, and wastes from manufacturing processes.

TAKING STRONGER MEASURES

Two years after the federal water-pollution law went into effect, the president's Water Resources Policy Commission issued a 445-page study that called for much stronger measures to deal with water regulation and pollution control. The country, according to the report, faced a "national peril in water waste." State and local governments had always set their own standards for waterways in their regions, and despite the problems, most state officials wanted to retain control over their own rivers and streams.

Noting in its report that separate antipollution plans for each state's section of the rivers was not working, the commission instead urged that plans be aimed at entire river basins, including streams and tributaries that flowed into the main waterways. The study also stressed the need for a national water policy that would apply to all state and local governments. President Truman, concurring with the call for federal action, said, "Plans for water development can no longer be made successfully by individual interests, whether they are private or public, whether they are local, state or Federal."

The commission report recommended that no new projects along major waterways be undertaken until a river-basin plan for every river had been adopted. "Grave as it is now, the pollution problem is bound to deepen as the population and industry grow," the report noted. Yet the loss of pure water to pollution was not irretrievable, according to the commission, provided immediate action was taken. The report stopped short of calling for federal control of rivers and streams. It concluded, however, that if "cooperative pollution control" among state, federal, and local governments did not succeed within ten years, Congress should revise the laws to allow the federal government to take over enforce-ment of antipollution regulations.

During the eight years the Water Pollution Control Act remained in effect, partnerships among local communities, states, and regional groups increased efforts to reduce water pollution. More than half the states strengthened their laws against polluters and adopted programs to protect water-ways. The lack of federal funds, however, hampered the push for clean water.

In 1955 the House Appropriations Committee refused to appropriate funds for enforcement of the 1948 act. Under the law, in order to deal with a pollution problem, all states involved, including the one causing the problem, had to agree to the steps to be taken. Only then could the secre-tary of health, education and welfare (HEW) take action. One congressman noted that the provision amounted to "a veto power by the offending state." At the end of 1955, the Natural Resources Council (NRC) criticized Congress for not allotting the funds. The federal government, NRC charged, "treated the [antipollution] program like a stepchild." The council saw the absence of a clear national policy and limits on federal authority as hindering progress in the campaign for clean water.

With the Water Pollution Control Act of 1956, Congress finally delivered funds and strengthened enforcement pro-visions. President Eisenhower, who had supported the ini-tial bill but opposed the construction grants, signed the act into law on July 9, 1956. The act provided up to $50 million a year for ten years in matching grants to build new treat-ment facilities—a welcome boost to cities and towns but only a fraction of the total price tag for the facilities. A House Public Works Committee report indicated that the cost of sewage-treatment plants and sewers needed to meet current demands could exceed $1.9 billion.

The 1956 law broke new ground in requiring states and municipalities to obtain federal approval for antipollution programs before receiving federal funds for wastewater-treatment projects. It also authorized the U.S. surgeon general, as the overseer of the nation's health, to recommend ways to decrease pollution in rivers and streams and enabled the attorney general to sue polluters. In each case, states would be consulted, and the "written consent of a state water pollution control agency" would be required in the event of a lawsuit. The *New York Times*, describing the new law as "still extremely tender toward states' rights," noted that at least states that polluted could no longer veto action to correct the problem.

Senator Edmund Muskie poses on the rocks along the Atlantic coast during his campaign for president in April 1971.

CHAPTER TWO

The Antipollution Warrior

Edmund S. Muskie arrived in Washington, D.C., in January 1959 as Maine's first Democratic senator since 1917. Margaret Chase Smith, the only female member of the Senate, filled Maine's other seat.

The Senate operated as an almost all-male sanctuary, bound by tradition, where those who had been in power the longest controlled things. Bound by tradition, members were expected to behave in accordance with rules that had been in place for a century and more. Speakers were expected to address one another politely and defer to other members when asked. Much of the work of both houses of Congress occurred behind the closed doors of committee meetings. No more than the occasional newspaper reporter sat in the gallery watching the day's business unfold. It was a major event when, in 1948, television cameras recorded a Senate hearing, that of the Senate Armed Services Committee, for the first time. Then in the 1950s Americans viewed mobsters testifying before Congress and saw Senator Joseph McCarthy and members of his committee closely examine witnesses during hearings (begun in the House during the late 1940s) to uncover alleged communist sympathizers in the U.S. Army. Everyday proceedings in the House were not televised until the late 1970s, however, and the more tradition-bound Senate held out against routine television coverage until 1986.

When Muskie arrived, powerful leaders controlled the Senate proceedings. Its majority leader, the Democrat Lyndon Johnson, ruled his party and the Senate with an iron hand. Combining flattery and intimidation, he persuaded Democrats to vote as he instructed them. During one of his first meetings with Muskie, Johnson told the freshman senator that at times Muskie might not know which way to vote and would decide only when "the clerk . . . gets to the M's." This was Johnson's way of making it clear that he expected to get Muskie's vote on an upcoming bill. Muskie, who had not yet made up his mind on the issue, replied, "The clerk hasn't gotten to the M's yet."

The young senator's show of independence did not sit well with Johnson. The majority leader ignored Muskie's top three committee choices—foreign relations, commerce, and judiciary—and instead assigned him to the Banking Committee (his fourth choice) and two minor committees, public works and government operations. As it turned out, the assignment to the Public Works Committee, which oversaw water and other natural resources, set the course of Muskie's Senate career. After this modest beginning, Muskie subsequently became chairman of the subcommittee on air and water pollution, from which position he put a national spotlight on the environment.

Senate Majority Leader Lyndon B. Johnson gazes out a window in 1955.

Edmund Muskie,

A reporter once described Edmund Sixtus Muskie, a senator from Maine, as "a cross between Abraham Lincoln and a moose." Six feet four inches tall, he had a long, craggy face, a large nose, big hands, and dark wavy hair. He loped rather than walked, bending his lanky frame slightly as he strode into a room. On formal occasions, he wore a bowtie and a dress shirt made by Hathaway, a Maine manufacturer. His flashing dark eyes betrayed a hot temper, which he used at times to his advantage—and at times left even his most loyal aides quaking. He also had the patience to consider complex problems and suggestions from all sides. "He could sit and wait until all the issues were raised, all the questions asked, and all the nonsense eliminated," recalled his longtime aide Leon Billings. "It was extraordinarily frustrating for conservatives; he could outwait them all."

Muskie was born on March 28, 1914, and grew up in Rumford, Maine, an industrial town near the Androscoggin River. The paper mill along the river's edge dominated the town and filled the sky over Rumford with smoke and the smell of rotten eggs. "We put up with the pollution," said a longtime Rumford resident, "because it provided jobs in the town. The entire town depended upon the company."

Muskie's father, Stephen (originally Marciszewski), emigrated from Poland at age seventeen and married Josephine Czarnecka, a woman from a Polish family in Buffalo, New York. The young couple settled in Rumford, where Stephen opened a tailor shop. Edmund was the second of six children.

The elder Muskie shared his love for nature with his children. On Wednesdays during the summer, when the merchants on Main Street closed their shops, he took them fishing in the nearby lakes, streams, and rivers. Muskie recalled catching landlocked salmon and trout in the clear

"Mr. Clean"

Maine waters. Years later, when Muskie made his case before the Senate for a law to protect the nation's waterways, salmon faced extinction in Maine rivers and many other regions of the country.

Muskie also learned politics from his father, one of the few businessmen in town who belonged to the Democratic Party. "When I worked in the [tailor] shop," Muskie wrote later, "I heard smoking-hot arguments, many of them with customers. A man might spend $500 or $1,000 a year with him, but if my father disagreed about politics, war, peace, prices, taxes, or whatever, they had it out. His opinions were worth more to him than his income."

The son acquired the father's political interests (they both admired Franklin D. Roosevelt, the first presidential candidate Edmund voted for). After class at Rumford High School, Muskie, a few other students, and their teacher stayed to discuss politics and history. He was elected class president, participated on the debate team, and later won a scholarship to Bates College in nearby Lewiston.

A brilliant student, Muskie graduated from Bates as a member of Phi Beta Kappa, the nation's oldest academic-honors fraternity, and earned a law degree from Cornell University Law School, in Ithaca, New York. He opened a law office in Maine, served in the navy during World War II, and won election to Maine's House of Representatives in 1946. In 1948 he married Jane Gray; they had five children.

In the spring of 1953 Muskie worked as a lobbyist in the legislature and served as a Democratic national committeeman. That summer he broke his back after falling down two flights of stairs while doing repairs on his Waterville home. He recuperated at the family camp on China Lake, swimming and thinking about his life. "That's when I began to have different ideas about what I ought to be involved in in politics," he recalled during a 1991 interview. He began to take a more active role in building the Democratic Party in Maine.

When Muskie first became involved in politics, Maine was an overwhelmingly Republican state. Not only did Maine Democrats hold no statewide office, but they put up only a handful of candidates in statewide races. In 1953 Muskie and other Maine Democrats circulated questionnaires all over the state to find out which issues concerned voters. They used the responses to create the party's platform. The action caught the attention of reporters and won high marks from the public as a refreshing new way of doing business. The following year voters elected Muskie governor; he was only the second Democrat to hold the post in the previous forty years. He served twenty-one years in the U.S. Senate, from 1959 to 1980, and won 60 percent or more of the vote in each election. In 1968 Muskie was Hubert Humphrey's running mate in their failed bid for the presidency and vice presidency. Muskie made his own run for the presidency four years later but failed to win the party's nomination. In 1980, as President Jimmy Carter's secretary of state, he negotiated the release of the U.S. hostages being held in Iran.

Muskie's Senate colleagues and others dubbed him Mr. Clean, partly for his work on the Clean Air and Clean Water Acts and partly for his reputation for integrity. One of the senator's greatest joys—according to his chief of staff Leon Billings, who helped draft both bills—was that he lived long enough to see salmon and trout come back to his favorite fishing holes in Maine. Their return, Billings noted, was a direct result of Muskie's own efforts to get the Clean Water Act passed.

NEW POLLUTION CONCERNS

Under the Water Pollution Control Act in 1956, many towns and cities used the federal funds the act allotted to begin building sewage-treatment plants, but water-pollution problems continued to concern scientists, health providers, and everyday citizens. In May 1961, 460 people who had eaten raw clams from Raritan Bay in New Jersey and New York developed hepatitis. The potentially life-threatening liver disease was linked to pollution from human waste in the bay. Sewage dumped in the Hudson River and sludge from sewage-treatment plants deposited offshore ended up in the bay and contaminated its waters with bacteria. The area had been closed to commercial shellfishing, but "pirate" diggers still collected clams from the area.

This and similar scares encouraged Congress to provide additional funds for treating and controlling waste. In 1961, amendments to the 1956 act increased funding for construction of treatment plants to $60 million in 1962, $90 million in 1963, and $100 million for each of the next four years.

In 1963 the Senate Public Works Committee set up a subcommittee on air and water pollution, with Senator Muskie as chairman. Muskie, a longtime proponent of environmental issues, used his new position to advance the antipollution cause throughout the 1960s and 1970s. As a boy, he had lived in a town where chemicals from the local paper company routinely polluted the air and the water. But he also fished in pure streams and camped in Maine's pristine woods. His interest in curbing pollution, he said, "began in my backyard" and sprang from a "desire to preserve the natural wonders of home. There may be no stronger motivation."

Even with pollution and its consequences frequently in the news, many people still had little knowledge of or interest in the problem. During a hearing in the 1960s focused on the Mississippi River, one government witness proposed to Muskie that the river be fenced in to keep people from tossing beer cans in it.

By 1963 the U.S. government was spending $90 million on municipal sewage-treatment plants and an additional

Industrial accidents in early 1963 caused large amounts of soybean oil and petroleum to run into streams along the Minnesota River and eventually into the Mississippi below St. Paul.

$2.5 million on the federal water-pollution program. Enforcement of water-pollution standards had been the responsibility of the U.S. Public Health Service since 1955. Noting the service's feeble attempts at enforcement, several congressmen proposed a bill to transfer responsibility to the Department of Health, Education and Welfare. The bill also allocated more money for municipal sewage-treatment plants and mandated federal water-quality standards. The last provision sparked a protest from the business community, which would have to bear the expense of setting up costly pollution-control systems.

One of the bill's House sponsors, John D. Dingell, a Democrat from Michigan, objected to an alternative plan to set up a bureau of environmental health within the Public Health Service. "The water pollution program is buried in the hierarchy [at Public Health Service]," Dingell said. "The Health Service is health-oriented rather than enforcement-oriented." He cited several instances of water pollution around the nation in urging members to pass the bill. "We need adequate water quality for all legitimate water uses," he said, "for public supplies, propagation of fish and wildlife, recreation purposes, and for agriculture and industrial uses."

In the Senate, Muskie introduced and managed the bill. Its opponents objected to federal control over water pollution. Senator John Sherman Cooper, a Kentucky Republican, argued that states should have a say in the treatment of their own water bodies and should participate in setting water-quality standards. The Senate rejected his amendment and then passed the Muskie plan on October 16, 1963. Though the *New York Times* applauded the bill's passage, two years went by before Congress acted on its authorization to set up another national agency to deal with dirty water.

Paper mill owned by the Fox River Paper Company in Appleton, Wisconsin, 1898.

CHAPTER THREE

Air Pollution
and Pesticides

Dirty water was not environmentalists' only concern. They worried about dirty air and contaminated soil,
too. Their first targets were fumes from burning wood and
from coal furnaces, which had been present in industrial
areas since the nineteenth century. Before 1850, several U.S.
cities had enacted laws to regulate factory smoke, though
their concerns were unpleasantness and unsightliness
rather than health. While there was early recognition that
dirty water was associated with disease, few people thought
smoky air a matter of health. Besides, airborne particulates
and gases remained invisible until weather conditions made
smog appear.

When World War II began, an ever-increasing number of
factories, workers, and automobiles came to the West Coast.
With them came smog, the soupy mix of smoke, fog, and
chemicals that obscures vision and irritates lungs. By 1943
the Los Angeles Bureau of Air Pollution Control was seeking

to deal with it. The district attorney sued a long list of manufacturers under the state's public-nuisance law to stop them
from polluting the air. His efforts failed to clear the skies.
A newspaper report declared that the city's motor vehicles
alone emitted nearly 3 billion cubic feet of exhaust gases
every day, with additional fumes coming from some 350,000
backyard incinerators and factories in neighboring towns.
The city's repeated "smog attacks" led California to pass the
Air Pollution Control District Act of 1947, which authorized
the state's counties to regulate local sources of air pollution. The law, the first of its type in the nation, encouraged
counties to join forces on a regional basis. Since dirty air had
become an irritant in much of the country, other states followed suit.

As the West Coast struggled with smog, Pittsburgh and
East Coast mill cities contended with smoke and coal dust.
In 1948 a dense cloud of sulfur dioxide and other pollutants
from steel mills hovered over Donora, Pennsylvania, for six
days. Nineteen died, and almost half of the town's population was sickened. Five years later smog settled over New
York City for a week. Also in 1953, heavy smog over Utah
caused a military jet to crash; smog was also blamed for several fatal multicar pileups on the New Jersey Turnpike.

Los Angeles could not free itself of smog despite efforts to
control burning and factory emissions. In 1954 Los Angeles
and its outlying suburbs suffered through ten days of choking, blinding smog. Reports later linked a rise in deaths from
lung cancer to cities plagued with heavy-smog problems.
These events and others led to a call for action by the federal
government.

In 1955, President Dwight D. Eisenhower, as part of a proposed national health program, asked Congress to allot funds

Mrs. John Long washes dirt off the face of her six-year-old son, Christopher, after a soot storm swept over a three-mile area of Philadelphia on June 22, 1953. The soot, which clung to hundreds of people, was traced to a generating plant at an electric company in the area. A company spokesman blamed the dirty air on the failure of the plant's soot-collecting device.

for a study of air pollution. He warned, "The atmosphere over some population centers may be approaching the limit of its ability to absorb air pollutants with safety to health." Congress declined to pass Eisenhower's overall health program, but it did enact the National Air Pollution Control Act, the first federal legislation to address the issue. The law provided the Public Health Service an annual research grant of $5 million for five years of study. Amendments to the law in 1960 extended the research grants for another four years. In 1962 amendments directed toward researching the effect of automobile emissions on health were enacted.

KILLING THE EARTH ALONG WITH THE BUGS

Concerns about DDT—one of several effective but toxic chemical pesticides used by farmers and gardeners—began to be voiced in the mid–1940s. Studies showed that the pesticides persisted in the air, water, and soil. Their danger came to wide public attention only after Rachel Carson, a biologist and science writer, wrote about them. In July 1962 the *New Yorker* presented Carson's work in serial form; two months later it was published as a book, *Silent Spring*, and became a best seller. "Can anyone believe it is possible to lay down such a barrage of poisons on the surface of the earth without making it unfit for all life?" Carson asked her readers. The human body, like other living organisms, she said, was susceptible to the invisible poisons in the air and water.

Her words raised an alarm across America, a warning that soon reached the halls of Congress. People began to realize that pollution could affect their health and that of their families. The national debate that ensued led to efforts to ban DDT and control pollution and gave birth to an environmental movement. It also sparked a furor among those who regarded its conclusions as alarmist. Farmers and industrialists pointed to the fact that DDT and other chemicals had made the United States the world's leading food producer. Dupont and other chemical companies appealed to American consumers, who had welcomed each of their new products, from unbreakable plastic storage containers to special glue. According to Carson's biographer Linda Lear, the chemical companies spent a quarter of a million dollars to dispute her research. Their efforts, however, did not succeed in discrediting Carson or her message.

President John F. Kennedy, impressed by Carson's book, called for a government investigation of the issues she

Rachel Carson, a pioneer in the conservationist movement, poses at her desk in Washington, D.C., on March 13, 1963. Carson's book, *Silent Spring*, drew attention to problems caused by agricultural pesticides.

raised. In June 1963 the presidential science committee issued a report that pesticide-spraying programs were "failures." Sympathetic lawmakers in statehouses and in Congress introduced bills to curb pollution. On June 6, 1963, Carson testified before the Senate Commerce Committee on the dangers of chemical pesticides. She said that pesticides increased in strength as they passed through the food chain. Carson's testimony came in support of two bills: one aimed at protecting fish and wildlife from pesticides and other chemical poisons, and the other establishing federal control over dangerous pesticides.

Carson joined forces with Senator Jacob K. Javits, a Republican from New York, in criticizing state and federal officials

Rachel Carson

Rachel Carson did not set out to be a crusader. A petite woman with the quiet air of a poet, Carson wrote three best sellers about the life of the sea before embarking on *Silent Spring*, the book that made her famous.

Born in Springdale, Pennsylvania, on May 27, 1907, Carson was the youngest of three children. Her mother taught her "the lore of birds, insects, and residents of streams and ponds." The family lived on sixty-five acres of land that overlooked the Allegheny River. Carson's first published work, written when she was ten, ran in *St. Nicholas*, a magazine for and by children. She majored in biology at Pennsylvania College for Women (later renamed Chatham College) and earned a master's degree in zoology from Johns Hopkins University. Carson later studied at Woods Hole Marine Biological Laboratory, in Massachusetts, and became a biologist, writer, and editor for the U.S. Bureau of Fisheries (later, the Fish and Wildlife Service). She also wrote magazine articles about science and the environment. An expanded version of one of these articles became her first book, *Under the Sea-Wind*, a lyrical exploration of the wonder and beauty of life beneath the ocean.

Silent Spring, a cautionary tale of the perils of pollution, propelled Carson into the limelight as a leader in the environmental cause. Her lyrical style, coupled with clearly presented scientific facts, captured readers' imagination. She described in detail the effects of DDT and other insecticides on the human body: how one poison led to instant paralysis and another caused tremors, muscle spasms, convulsions, and death. *Silent Spring* opens with a fable of a bucolic American town suddenly destroyed by a "strange blight" that turns out to be chemical pollution. The image of the little town and the menace that left it withered and silent stuck with readers. Carson's book, like no other, made the American public acutely aware of the dangers of pollution.

The *New Yorker*'s publication of *Silent Spring* in 1962 prompted bags of letters from concerned Americans. One writer, concerned about food contaminated by hydrocarbons, asked Carson what she ate. "Chlorinated hydrocarbons, like everyone else," she replied.

In 1963 Carson told a television reporter that the public's attitude toward nature was "critically important" because mankind had the ability to alter and destroy the natural world. "Man is a part of nature, and his war against nature is inevitably a war against himself," she said. "We in this generation must come to terms with nature, and I think we're challenged as mankind has never been challenged before to prove our maturity and our mastery, not of nature, but of ourselves."

Carson's work inspired the modern environmental movement and led Americans to see dangers in the air and water around them. In the 1960s the U.S. Fish and Wildlife Service established a wildlife refuge that now occupies more than nine thousand acres along fifty miles (80 km) of the southern coast of Maine. It is named in Carson's honor.

As a result of Carson's book, the President's Science Advisory Committee launched a study of pesticides. The committee's report reached the same conclusions Carson had. In 1964, at age fifty-six, Carson died of breast cancer. The United States banned DDT in 1972 and adopted many of the safeguards Carson had urged.

for failing to notify property owners in New York and New Jersey of pesticide spraying in their area to kill gypsy moths. Sevin, a powerful insecticide, had been sprayed over more than 100,000 acres in the two-state area. DDT was also used on wooded areas. Carson, in testimony before the Senate, lobbied for a regulation requiring that landowners be given advance notice of spraying so that they could protest if they wanted to. Every citizen, she told Congress, had "the right . . . to be secure in his own home against the intrusion of poisons applied by other persons." Noting that doctors did not yet know the extent of medical problems caused by the poisons, she urged Congress to limit the use of such chemicals; she also criticized the American Medical Association for relying on data from pesticide trade organizations in answering patients' concerns.

Less than a month after Carson's April 1964 death from breast cancer, on May 12, 1964, President Lyndon B. Johnson signed into law a bill that established more stringent federal regulations of pesticides. Under the law, new pesticides could not be sold on the U.S. market until cleared by the Agriculture Department. Previous regulations had allowed manufacturers to sell pesticides "under protest" even after they failed to meet safety standards. In signing the bill, Johnson expressed gratitude for Carson's work on the issue. "We owe much to her and to those who still work for the cause of a safer and healthier America," he said.

"THE AIR WE BREATHE"

For many Americans, the 1960s marked a turning point in their view of air pollution. Seeing Rachel Carson's attack on pesticides and the gains made in wastewater treatment, they began to think about improving air quality. Until that time, most people, if they thought about air pollution at all, viewed it as the price to be paid for technology—in particular, the automobile. "The notion that you could somehow prevent the escape of gases into the atmosphere and yet continue the functions that produced them had been inconceivable," Edmund Muskie wrote in his autobiography, *Journeys*.

In January 1963 Senator Abraham Ribicoff, a Democrat from Connecticut, introduced a bill that, for the first time, gave the federal government the power to take action against air polluters. Ribicoff told his fellow senators, "Now is the time for action. Millions of sensible men, women and children are trapped in our growing cities today. They are forced to breathe polluted air, and they usually don't know they are doing so." Furthermore, the surgeon general said researchers had produced evidence that linked air pollution to a variety of respiratory diseases, which cost $7 billion every year.

Modeled on the Senate's 1963 water-pollution control legislation, the clean-air bill called for establishment of air-quality standards and provided money for research and for the formation of local and regional control agencies. After the House passed its version of the bill, it proceeded to the Senate, where experts testified that the bill needed to address invisible pollutants from industrial and chemical wastes in addition to smoke. In September Senator Muskie and several other government officials took a helicopter tour of New York City and neighboring New Jersey. After viewing the billowing smoke of industrial and city incineration plants from the air, Muskie told reporters that the nation's air pollution "far outstretches our efforts to do anything about it."

Despite his comment, Muskie's committee released a sixty-two-page report that linked air pollution to cancer, emphysema, and other diseases and claimed that atmospheric conditions could transform air pollutants into even more dangerous chemicals.

On December 10, 1963, Congress passed the first Clean Air Act. The act provided federal money for pollution research, encouraged states to form pollution-control agencies, and gave the federal government authority to get involved in pollution disputes between states. Control of air pollution, however, remained in the states' hands.

POINTING A FINGER AT AUTOMOBILES

As early as the 1940s, scientists had identified automobiles as a cause of dirty air, but it was not until the 1960s that they were included in clean-air legislation. California, home of the nation's worst smog, enacted the first laws regulating auto emissions and requiring installation of an emission-control device on all new cars as of 1961. The device, which cost about $4 per car, reduced pollution from emissions by about 35 percent. New York followed suit in 1963. As a result of the two states' laws, manufacturers began equipping all new cars with the device on January 1, 1964.

In 1965 Muskie's Senate Subcommittee on Air and Water Pollution decided to extend these auto-emissions laws to the country as a whole. "We wanted to require compliance with federal standards," he wrote later, "because automobiles do not stay in one jurisdiction and because we believed it was a national problem." Both President Lyndon Johnson and the secretary of health, education and welfare, Anthony Celebrezze, called for a federal law to control automobile emissions. "Considering the present extent of the automotive air-pollution [problem] and the speed at which it is growing, effective control of these emissions is needed now," Celebrezze said in a January 1965 report to Congress.

Smog, a form of air pollution caused mainly by automobiles and industrial manufacturing plants, shrouds the sky over downtown Los Angeles in the late 1960s.

Senator Muskie formally introduced the bill in January as an amendment to the Clean Air Act of 1963. Twenty senators, both Democrats and Republicans, cosponsored the bill. Representative Seymour Halpern, a New York Republican, presented a similar bill in the House. His bill called for a federal law requiring that within eighteen months all automobiles be equipped with devices to control their exhaust.

While the Halpern bill made its way through the House, the Senate bill went to the air and water pollution subcommittee for review. Muskie chaired the hearings with enthusiasm and framed questions to get the information he sought. Having studied the topic beforehand, he knew exactly what needed to be covered during the hearings.

OPPONENTS TAKE AIM

A string of mill owners, auto manufacturers, oil and gas companies, and other businesses prepared to testify against the measures. They presented two major arguments: (1) the proponents' research was faulty and thus the problem was not as severe as claimed, and (2) pollution could not be controlled without endangering jobs and putting firms out of business. The Johnson administration, taking both positions, at some times pushed for strict controls and at others agreed with industry assessments.

In testimony before the committee in April, administration officials supported the committee's findings that automobile emissions caused serious air-pollution problems nationwide. But they balked at the committee's proposed deadlines to require automobile manufacturers to install devices to control emissions. An HEW official testified that the bill should be postponed at least a year while the government conducted further research on air pollution. The HEW and Interior secretaries, in letters to the committee, criticized the bill as "too restrictive." President Johnson wanted the committee to work out a voluntary deal with the auto industry.

Since Johnson's proposal would have gutted the bill, it enraged environmentalists and even some government officials who administered the government's antipollution programs. One expert testified that California's pollution-control board recognized the need for more research but believed the problem was too serious to wait "20 or 30 years for every fact to [be] established." This witness recommended that the federal government follow California's example and enact the regulations. "Air pollution is critical enough in many parts of the country to warrant an accelerated program."

Muskie took the hearings to Detroit and questioned industry spokesmen on their home ground. The automobile makers testified that scientists needed to conduct much more research before the need for controls on auto emissions could be established but also said that they could install devices to control emissions on 1968 car models if Congress should require them to do it. Muskie pursued this concession when writing the final legislation.

BILL WINS SUPPORT

While Congress considered the final bill, others led their own campaigns against air pollution and the auto industry. In June, James M. Quigley, assistant secretary of HEW, testified in New York City that air pollution cost the nation $11 billion annually in damage to buildings, clothing, paint, and crops and in other expenses. The figure did not take into account illnesses or deaths caused by dirty air. In 1965 Ralph Nader's book *Unsafe at Any Speed* detailed the unsafe features of U.S. automobiles and their contribution to air pollution. The controversy generated by Nader's book led to increased support for federal controls on auto emissions and the passage of auto-safety standards.

On May 10, 1965, the Senate's pollution subcommittee approved the clean air bill with several changes. In his original bill, Muskie included specific standards for auto emissions and a deadline to have them in place by November 1, 1966. Under pressure from the Johnson administration, the subcommittee dropped both requirements. Instead, the bill gave HEW the power to determine the standards. Muskie privately arranged with HEW, however, to adopt standards similar to those used in California. On May 14 the Public Works Committee accepted the subcommittee's report and sent the bill to the full Senate, where it passed on May 18. The bill received House approval at the end of September, and the Senate accepted the House version a week later. President Johnson signed it into law on October 20, 1965.

The final version of the bill—the Clean Air Act Amendments and Solid Waste Disposal Act—ordered HEW to create standards for automobile and truck emissions and issue regulations to enforce them. Congress set no specific deadline, but HEW officials said they expected the regulations to take effect by September 1, 1967. The legislation also set up a federal laboratory to conduct research on air-pollution control and authorized $40 million for cities and states to build non-polluting solid-waste-disposal plants. For the first time, Congress gave the federal government authority over individual states to see that air pollution regulations were obeyed.

Over the next four years Congress amended the Clean Air Act three more times. The 1966 amendments expanded programs set up by local authorities. In 1967 Congress passed the much more comprehensive Air Quality Act (also known as the Clean Air Act of 1967); it amended the 1963 act and gave the federal government the power to develop clean-air programs if states did not put their own in place quickly. Only California won the right to run its own program, since it was even more restrictive than the one proposed in the new federal law.

HEW was directed to set up air-quality regions in areas where pollution affected more than one state. Although several state officials protested that the act infringed on states' rights, the measure won unanimous congressional support. Congress, however, turned down President Johnson's request for national air-quality standards. Further amendments, passed in 1969, set aside money for research into fuels and automobiles with reduced emissions.

CHAPTER FOUR

The Era of the Environment

During the six years Lyndon Johnson was president (1963–1969), Congress passed more than fifteen laws related to pollution and the environment. In addition, Lady Bird Johnson, the first lady, made enhancing the environment her mission. She spent many hours touring communities, planting trees and flowers, and urging people to care for their natural surroundings.

Her advocacy inspired Congress to pass the Highway Beautification Act in 1965, which limited billboards along federal highways, called for screening of nearby junkyards and other unscenic areas, and provided funds for landscaping along the roads.

Lady Bird Johnson's campaign to beautify America went beyond trees and plants. "It involves much more: clean water, clean air, clean roadsides, safe waste disposal and preservation of valued old landmarks as well as great parks and wilderness areas," she said. "To me . . . beautification means our

Lady Bird Johnson (*in pink shirt and cowboy hat*) leads a tour of the Big Bend National Park on April 2, 1966, during her national beautification campaign.

total concern for the physical and human quality we pass on to our children and the future."

Her crusade for a more beautiful America helped focus attention on the environment. "The environment is where we all meet," she once said, "where all have a mutual interest; it is the one thing all of us share. It is not only a mirror of ourselves, but a focusing lens on what we can become."

A NEW WATER-CLEANUP BILL

Over the course of two years, 1963 to 1965, Senator Muskie's Subcommittee on Air and Water Pollution held hearings across the country on pollution in U.S. waterways. These hearings and the horror stories that emerged from them about the dangers of dirty water led to demands for government action. Hundreds of thousands of citizens in Ohio petitioned for a cleanup of Lake Erie. An outbreak of stomach disorders in California raised concerns over the effectiveness of sewage-treatment systems. Pollution-related water shortages in the northeast further increased public agitation.

Using information from the hearings, the committee issued a report, "Steps toward Clean Water," and began drafting another new bill. On January 28, 1965, the Senate passed the new proposals by a vote of 68 to 8. The final bill, the Federal Water Quality Act, which was signed by President Johnson in October 1965, created another new federal agency, the Federal Water Pollution Control Administration. It operated under the HEW Department until 1966, when it became part of the Interior Department.

"No one has the right to use America's waterways, which belong to all the people, as a sewer," Johnson said in signing the bill. The 1965 legislation required all states to set water-quality standards for their rivers, streams, and other bodies of water within their borders. The law for the first time gave the federal government power to establish standards for states that did not set their own by the federal deadline. The law also provided grants for research and improvement of antipollution facilities. The measure aimed to prevent pollution as well as to deal with areas already affected by it.

The act's antipollution measures, however, were "barely sufficient to enable the nation to hold its own in the struggle for pure water," according to a *New York Times* editorial. Just one new treatment plant cost $50 million, half the amount the federal government allotted for the nation annually. Muskie, chief Senate sponsor and author of the bill, acknowledged that Congress's work in the campaign against pollution had just begun.

The law signaled a major shift by placing more emphasis on prevention. The new policies made state and local governments and private industries responsible for removing pollution from wastewater before discharging it into waterways.

A RELUCTANT PARTNERSHIP

Through the six New England states, including Muskie's state of Maine, flowed some of America's dirtiest rivers, owing in part to the manufacturing plants and other industries concentrated in the region. New England's various state officials resisted federal attempts to develop and run cleanup programs. New Hampshire threatened to arrest Public Health Service agents who were studying pollution in the state's oyster beds. Maine questioned whether federal HEW agents had jurisdiction, and Massachusetts set aside some streams unsuitable for swimming as sewage canals. "We've proceeded on the principle of making a stream suitable for what it is to be used for—not to provide the highest water quality," said Worthen H. Taylor, chief engineer of the Massachusetts Department of Public Health. "Our theory is that you don't provide the quality of water in these places for uses it can't be used for."

The extent of wastewater and industrial pollution and the cost of treating and cleaning it up began to change minds. Some industrialists who had long resisted federal interference came to accept the inevitability of federal control. For

their part, some activists saw that their opponents' coopera-
tion was essential. Senator Muskie saw his task as getting
"the environmentalist to see that commerce and industry
have to live, if we are to live; and [getting] the commercial
or industrial man to see that no one will live, work, or profit,
including him, if there is not a satisfactory world in which to
do so."

James M. Quigley, the assistant secretary of HEW, was less
conciliatory. "Unless American industry really adjusts to the
fact that pollution control is a regular part of overhead, we're
not going to get the kind of action we need," he told reporters
after the enactment of the 1965 water-quality law. "Also," he
said, "this is the states' last big opportunity to do their part
in this job. If they do it, water pollution control will be truly
a Federal-state-local partnership. If the states fail, the tro-
phy is going to the Federal Government by default. Nineteen
sixty-six is the key year on this."

NEW PROPOSALS

At the beginning of 1966, municipal plants provided adequate sewage treatment for only about one-third of Americans. Secondary treatment facilities—those that processed
waste twice—removed up to 90 percent of the bacteria
and other contaminants in wastewater. Yet Detroit and
many other large cities used basic sewage systems, which
removed only large chunks of waste. In New York 400,000
gallons of untreated sewage were released each day.

Many cities and towns lacked the tax revenue to build
better treatment plants, and President Johnson and Congress set out to provide federal help. The proposed River
Basin Clean Rivers Act targeted a number of river basins for
cleanup. Congress broadened the measure's scope to make

it the Clean Water Restoration Act of 1966. The act provided $3.5 billion in federally generated revenue to cities, towns, and states for the construction of sewage-treatment facilities. The final figure represented a compromise between the House, which called for $2.45 billion, and the Senate, which asked for $6 billion.

Congress also addressed the problem of oil-contaminated water in amendments to the Oil Pollution Act of 1924. The original Senate version of the bill called for much stronger measures against oil polluters than were enacted. It increased the maximum fines from $2,500 (in the 1924 law) to $10,000. The Senate bill also expanded federal involvement in clean-ups and litigation. The measure covered inland waterways (rivers and lakes) as well as coastal waters. It applied the regulations both to shippers and to onshore manufacturers and oil-tank operations.

In the face of widespread opposition to this bill, however, members of a joint conference shaped a compromise that could win support in both the Senate and the House. Conference members eliminated land-based polluters from the bill and approved an amendment that redefined "oil discharges" from the original version's "any accidental, negligent, or willful spilling" to "any grossly negligent, or willful spilling." The compromise bill passed the House and Senate, and President Johnson signed it on November 3, 1966.

While the clean-water bill allocated revenue to build new sewage-treatment plants, those who were eager to punish the people they judged responsible for oil discharges were disappointed. The "grossly negligent or willful" restriction made the punitive aspects of the law practically unenforceable. Since only crew members usually witnessed a spill, it was impossible to prove that those responsible had been grossly negligent. In April 1967 the Justice Department reported that since the passage of the amendment, it had not filed one lawsuit against offending shipowners (the department had earlier averaged at least a hundred suits a year). The author of the revised definition, Texas Democratic Congressman James C. Wright Jr., said he had not intended to block enforcement of the law but merely wanted to help "the poor little devil who might have [discharged oil] accidentally."

When efforts to revise the law failed, Muskie and others presented a bill that dealt with liability for oil spills. When this 1968 Senate bill, the Water Quality Improvement Act, reached the House, representatives tacked on amendments that, in Muskie's opinion, gutted it. At the time, Muskie was campaigning for vice president on the Democratic ticket. From aboard his plane, he sent word that he opposed the changes to the bill. Congress adjourned before an agreement could be reached.

BEGINNING OF A MOVEMENT

Despite tough state laws against pollution, residents of Denver rarely got a good view of the Rocky Mountains, only fifteen miles away but obscured by smog. Scientists meeting in the spring of 1966 reported that every U.S. city emitted "as much particulate matter as a volcano." Later that year the National Academy of Sciences described the pollution problem as "unprecedented and becoming desperate." Its report predicted that by 1980 pollutants from power plants would double and sewage would deplete the nation's twenty-two largest rivers of oxygen during the dry season; by 2000 sewage too would double. In addition, household waste was increasing by 4 percent each year, chemicals in the air were causing crop damages estimated at $325 million annually,

Burn, River,

On June 22, 1969, flames erupted along the oil-slicked sludge on the surface of the Cuyahoga River and burned a railroad bridge before local fire crews could put it out. The fire caused about $50,000 in damages, but the river had seen worse. In 1952 a similar incident—caused when oil slicks on the water caught fire— destroyed a shipyard and resulted in damages exceeding $1.5 million.

The 1969 blaze captured the attention of *Time* magazine, which described the burning river as "chocolate-brown, oily, bubbling with subsurface gases," a waterway that "oozes rather than flows." Songwriter Randy Newman used the image of the burning river in his 1972 song "Burn On":

> Cleveland, even now I can remember
> 'Cause the Cuyahoga River
> Goes smokin' through my dreams
> Burn on, big river, burn on.

The image of the burning Cuyahoga came to represent all of America's pollution-filled rivers and generated support for the Clean Water Act and similar measures.

After the fire, Cuyahoga River conservation groups counted only two species of fish in the river. In the summer of 2008, thirty-nine years later, biologists from the Environmental Protection Agency (EPA) found forty species of fish there. "It's been an absolutely amazing recovery," said Steve Tuckerman of EPA's Ohio branch. "I wouldn't have believed that this section of the river would have this dramatic of a turnaround in my career, but it has."

Just as the river's fire became a potent symbol of the nation's polluted waterways, so did its recovery serve as an example of the rebirth of American rivers and streams since the enactment of the Clean Water Act of 1972.

Burn

A fire tug fights flames on the Cuyahoga River near downtown Cleveland, Ohio, where oil and other industrial wastes caught fire on June 25, 1952. A similar fire on the Cuyahoga in 1969 helped inspire Earth Day.

In a 1967 photograph (*held in hand below*), old junk cars, used to stop erosion, line the banks of the Cuyahoga River in Brecksville, Ohio. In the background is the same stretch of river—with trees and grasses lining the clear water—on April 21, 2006.

and automobile emissions were temporarily blinding drivers and causing fatal accidents as well as threatening residents' health. Other distressing statistics and predictions described rivers in New Jersey too dirty for boaters, fertilizer-fouled drinking water in the West, and contaminated beaches on both coasts. Gloomiest of all was the prediction that Lake Michigan and Lake Superior might be completely destroyed in fifteen years unless things changed quickly.

Pollution from four food-processing plants in Thonotosassa, Florida, killed 26 million fish in 1969, the largest fish kill ever recorded. In June of that year, oil slicks on the Cuyahoga River near Cleveland, Ohio, ignited. As flames shot five stories high, Congressman Louis Stokes described the river as the only one in the world "legally declared a fire hazard."

As one disaster followed another, Senator Gaylord Nelson, a Democrat from Wisconsin who had long championed environmental causes, sought to "put the environment into the political spotlight once and for all." He and Representative Paul N. McCloskey Jr., a California Republican, organized a national day to honor the earth and its resources. Nelson envisioned a day of national "teach-ins," during which Americans would study the effects of pollution on the environment. This day, Earth Day, has been called the beginning of the modern environmental movement.

An astounding 20 million Americans, including four thousand groups devoted to environmental issues, participated in the first Earth Day, April 22, 1970. Nelson believed it marked "a turning point in American history." Earth Day, he said, "may be the birth date of a new American ethic that rejects the frontier philosophy that the continent was put here for our plunder, and accepts the idea that even urbanized, affluent, mobile societies are interdependent with

Senator Gaylord Nelson (*right*) makes a point in June 1972 as Senator Walter F. Mondale, a Minnesota Democrat (*left*), and Senator James L. Buckley, a Conservative from New York (*center*), listen at the Capitol in June 1972. Nelson helped spearhead the first Earth Day.

the fragile, life-sustaining systems of the air, the water, the land." *American Heritage* magazine described the event as "one of the most remarkable happenings in the history of democracy."

Earth Day presented Americans with the specter of a dead earth, "increasingly incapable of forgiving what man has inflicted upon it," according to a report in *Time*. Most Americans saw Earth Day as a reminder that natural resources needed to be protected. Congress adjourned for the day to allow its members to participate in Earth Day events in their home districts. Some people had picnics, sang "Happy Earth

Day to you," planted shrubs and flowers, enjoyed the sunshine, and celebrated the earth's beauty.

The holiday captured the imagination of the nation's youth. *Time* reported that ten thousand students at fifteen hundred college campuses marked the day by participating in community cleanup projects, teach-ins, and similar programs. Throughout the nation the day was set aside to clean roadsides of litter. In New York City, Fifth Avenue was closed to traffic for two hours as 100,000 people walked down the thoroughfare. People rode bicycles, horses, and electric-powered buses to rallies.

Demonstrators conducted protests at a few notorious pollution sites. Students carrying filled trash bags stood on the banks of the Cuyahoga River in Cleveland, while another student, dressed as the city's founder, rowed to shore and declared that the locale was "too dirty to build a colony." In Kentucky's Appalachia region, twelve hundred students buried a casket filled with trash to protest that area's industrial pollution. A group gathered in front of Con Edison headquarters in New York City brandishing dead fish and shouting, "You're next, people!" The utility, the city's main supplier of gas and electric power, had been implicated in fish kills in the Hudson River.

The success of Earth Day caught the attention of politicians. Two Republican governors, Nelson Rockefeller of New York and William Cahill of New Jersey, ordered the creation of state-level environmental departments. At the urging of Democratic State Senator Robert Wetmore, Massachusetts added article 97 to its constitution in 1972. The article guaranteed citizens "the right to clean air and water, freedom from excessive and unnecessary noise, and the natural, scenic, historic, and esthetic qualities of their environment."

College students from the University of California at Irvine observe the first official Earth Day on April 22, 1970, by touring a garbage dump. The poster on the trolley reads, "Recognize the Polluter, Recognize Ourselves."

Illinois, Rhode Island, Texas, and Pennsylvania added similar "environmental bills of right" to their constitutions.

Earth Day's supporters made gains in the antipollution campaign. Shortly after the first Earth Day, a Louis Harris poll found that 54 percent of Americans said that they would support an increase in taxes to help remedy water and air pollution. Three years earlier, a majority of those polled had opposed paying more taxes for this cause.

NEW TOOLS TO PROTECT THE ENVIRONMENT

With politicians from the president on down viewing environmental issues as a road to public approval, the federal government's role in environmental matters changed. In late December 1969, Congress passed the National Environmental Policy Act (NEPA). With this law, Congress established a new federal policy of encouraging the "productive and enjoyable harmony between man and his environment" and called on the federal government to help protect the environment and public health.

The law created a Council on Environmental Quality (CEQ) to advise the president on issues related to the environment and required any new federal project to submit a report on its probable effect on the environment before it got started. This environmental-impact statement had to be reviewed by the CEQ and all other relevant departments, including state and local agencies. The law gave citizens the right to seek court orders to stop any project without such a statement.

President Richard M. Nixon signed the National Environmental Policy Act on January 1, 1970. The 1970s, he said, "absolutely must be the years when America pays its debt to the past by reclaiming the purity of its air, its waters and our living environment. It is literally now or never."

A *New York Times* columnist, James Reston, noted that the law gave Americans a new way of protecting the environment. "The American people finally have a personal and political issue they can do something about—if they're really serious," he said. Citizens had always been able to vote out unsympathetic politicians, but now, if they organized, there was a law they could use. "They [citizens] have practical power in both the industrial and political world, if they will organize at the local level," Reston wrote.

In July the president announced a plan to reorganize the federal government's many environmental agencies. The plan set up a single office, the Environmental Protection Agency (EPA), to handle air and water pollution, pesticide poisoning, and other environmental issues. The new agency took over the duties of the Interior Department's Federal Water Quality Administration and HEW's National Air Pollution Control Administration, as well as those of other offices that dealt with pesticides, radiation, and solid waste.

A thick blanket of smog covers New York City on July 29, 1970, in this view from the roof of the RCA Building in midtown Manhattan. The haze caused problems in cities all along the eastern seaboard from New York City to Atlanta. The tall building on the right is the Empire State Building.

CHAPTER FIVE

Clean Air Act of 1970

Earth Day and the plans leading up to it fueled a push for even stronger antipollution measures. Previous federal laws had actually accomplished little, and the regional approach had not worked. In the 1967 law, Congress called for more than one hundred air-quality regions to be established, but fewer than three dozen were in place by 1970. Although several states had strict laws, not one state had developed a complete program for controlling pollution.

Congress and President Nixon proposed new laws to help clean the air and water. In a February 1970 message, the president asked Congress to establish national air-quality standards, impose fines of up to $10,000 a day on polluters, and set goals for dramatically reduced auto emissions by 1980. "Air is our most vital resource," Nixon told Congress, "and its pollution is our most serious environmental problem."

In the House Representative Paul Rogers cosponsored a bill that duplicated most of Nixon's proposals. Under the bill, national air-quality standards would apply to all states, although individual states could adopt tougher regulations if they chose to do so. Rogers led the floor fight and served on the House Subcommittee on Health and Environment, which held hearings on the bill. Rogers, a conservative Democrat from Florida, told his colleagues, "We know what can be done, and we should do it."

During hearings on the legislation, supporters brought in people with ailments caused by air pollutants to tell their stories. The weather also helped win support for the measure: a choking smog blanketed Washington that spring and summer. "That kind of drove it home to Congress," recalled Rogers, whose committee united behind the bill. On June 10 the bill passed the House on a 374 to 1 vote. The final draft set aside $675 million over three years to administer the bill's provisions and to fund research.

The Senate's version of the bill incorporated Nixon's proposals but further toughened air-quality standards, set deadlines and fines, and increased the funding to $1.19 billion. With Senator Muskie guiding the legislation through his Air and Water Pollution Subcommittee and later through the Senate debate, it soon became known as the Muskie Bill.

The Muskie subcommittee conducted hearings on the bill in March 1970, as planners pulled together their final arrangements for the Earth Day celebrations. Francis Sargent, the governor of Massachusetts, was among many who addressed the subcommittee about the need for federal action on air pollution. "Many State health officials who had opposed the Clean Air Act of 1967 as an encroachment on their duties would now like to see even greater Federal involvement in air pollution control," he said. Though gains had been made in the campaign to clean the air, "the problem is growing faster than our efforts to control it are moving forward." National standards on fuel, air quality, automobile emissions, and other factors related to air pollution would actually help industry, the governor said, by providing a single set of regulations that applied to all, instead of a jumble of state laws. For example, Sargent said, "It is unreasonable to expect oil companies to supply fuel of different composition in each of 50 states. That would be a nightmare."

The bill had opponents. During the House debate, one of them quoted a small-town mayor's view that tough environmental laws threatened economic growth. "If you want this town to grow," the mayor had said, "it has got to stink." Muskie said that when he was governor of Maine in the 1950s, the opposite was true. One company had explored building a manufacturing plant along a Maine river but withdrew its proposal after learning that the river was so polluted it could not absorb any more industrial wastes.

Representatives from industry, the steelworkers union, the national chamber of commerce, and various environmental groups testified at the hearings. During the second day of testimony, the vice president of the giant chemical company Du Pont brought an experimental car to Washington, one designed to operate with practically no emissions.

THREE APPROACHES

Muskie wanted the new law's premise to be that the federal government had a duty to protect the public's health; he would then design the legislation to accomplish that goal. Other subcommittee members, among them Howard Baker and Thomas Eagleton (a Democrat from Missouri), had different approaches. Baker wanted to push the development of better technology to improve air quality; Eagleton, a former state attorney general, was concerned about the law's enforcement and so urged that the bill include deadlines for compliance.

All three approaches combined to form the Clean Air Act, as the legislation came to be called. What would it take, Muskie asked, for an automobile not to pose a threat to the public's health? One answer, provided by the director of the National Air Pollution Control Administration, was to reduce its emissions by 90 percent. Liking that answer, Muskie modified the bill to require carmakers to reduce toxic emissions by 90 percent in their 1975 and 1976 models—much sooner than anyone had expected. Urged on by Muskie and Baker, the members of the subcommittee approved the more stringent requirements. The vote, like the meetings, was held behind closed doors, which was standard procedure at the time.

The regulations added by the bill to the 1967 Clean Air Act:

- Established air-quality standards for six substances: lead, ozone, carbon monoxide, particulates (tiny pieces of airborne matter), nitrogen dioxide, and sulfur dioxide. The EPA was given the authority to ban emissions of hazardous substances altogether.
- Gave automakers five years to produce a car that emitted almost no pollutants. Under the law, auto manufacturers would have to reduce hydrocarbon and carbon monoxide emissions by 90 percent in all 1975 model cars and nitrous oxide emissions in every 1976 model. Automakers were allowed a one-year extension in later revisions of the bill.
- Phased out the use of lead in gasoline.
- Required all new manufacturing facilities and old

Senator Edmund Muskie (*center*) and Senator Warren Magnuson (*right*) examine the battery system in an experimental electric car produced by General Motors, outside the Senate Office Building in Washington, D.C., on March 13, 1967.

plants undergoing major changes to use the "best available" technology in controlling pollution.

• Required states to submit plans to control air pollution and meet federal air-quality standards. Under the law states had nine months to develop their plans after HEW issued the standards. They would then have five and a half years to implement them.

• Imposed fines on violators as high as $10,000 a day in civil penalties and $25,000 a day in criminal penalties, plus two years in jail. The federal government had authority to shut down operations that violated the law.

• Allowed citizens to sue polluters and government agencies to force them to take action.

- Gave the EPA broad powers to enforce the law, including filing suit against polluters if the U.S. attorney general failed to do so.

These changes gave the federal government the power to set standards that both industry and the states would have to meet. The bill also set deadlines, something Congress had never done before, and allowed lawsuits by citizens to force compliance. Usually Congress passed a law outlining a general policy, and federal agencies drew up regulations to fulfill the policy. In the Clean Air Act, Congress required the EPA to draw up specific regulations and enforce fixed deadlines. "The bill took out the 'may' words and put in 'must' words," said Leon Billings, Muskie's chief of staff.

Carmakers in 1970 did not have the technology to reduce emissions by 90 percent, as the bill required. Senator Baker believed that American ingenuity could solve the problem and that businesses should be required to adopt new technology to reduce emissions. By setting such a high standard, he claimed, the law would set in motion the research and development of new technologies. This tactic resurfaced in later legislation.

Companies that failed to develop and use new technology to fulfill the law's requirement were at the mercy of Congress. Unlike most other legislation, the Clean Air Act gave Congress a direct hand in creating specific regulations instead of simply allowing the EPA to draw up rules that met the law's provisions. "Everyone understood that the goal could not be reached with state-of-the-art technology, but the debate was not over the 90 percent cut. It was over what could be done if the automobile industry could not meet the standard," said Billings. "Muskie's theory was that a bureaucrat would always extend the deadline, so he wanted Congress to make the decision."

Muskie issued the subcommittee's report on the bill shortly before Congress's summer break in August 1970. The automobile industry charged that his changes radically transformed the measure and demanded new hearings. After Congress returned from vacation, the chief executive officers of the auto companies came to Washington—the first time in memory that such a thing had happened—to discuss the bill in Muskie's office. The meeting did not go well, Billings said. "They [the auto executives] came in and expressed outrage that Congress would have the temerity to tell them how to build cars, and it was a very contentious meeting. But all that meeting did, I think, was steel [Muskie's] resolve." After the meeting E. N. Cole, the president of General Motors, told Muskie that his company could not meet the act's deadline. "As far as we now know," he wrote, "[it] simply is not technologically possible within the time frame required."

The subcommittee met with various groups to discuss the changes in the bill. As a result, the panel approved a one-year extension if the auto emissions standards could not be met because pertinent technology had not yet been developed. The auto-emissions standards and fines remained in the bill, however, despite strong opposition from the auto industry and the Nixon administration.

When Senator Robert P. Griffin, a Republican whose Michigan district included many in the auto industry, complained about the bill's cost, Muskie countered, "Where would the Senator place a decision of such importance to the public health? In the boards of directors of these great motor companies? Does Congress have no responsibility?"

On September 22, after only two days of debate on the

Senate floor, the bill passed unanimously, 73 to 0. Those against the measure did not vote. Politicians did not want to go on record as opposing any popular legislation, especially right before an election. Senator Eugene McCarthy, a Democrat from Minnesota, commented to Muskie after the vote, "Ed, you finally found an issue better than motherhood—and some people are even against motherhood."

After the Senate passed its version of the bill, the matter went to a joint House-Senate conference. The two stumbling blocks to agreement were the Senate's auto-emissions standards and the provision that allowed citizens to file suit against polluters. Just before the November elections, Muskie persuaded the House members to accept the Senate's standards. Shortly after the elections, President Nixon announced that he would oppose the legislation. At that point, the House Republicans at the joint conference withdrew their approval of the deal, according to Billings.

Muskie believed that power lay in the middle ground between the radical left and the conservative right. He saw himself as the man in the middle. He took that position at the conference meeting called to decide the fate of the Clean Air Act. First, he rallied the support of the Democrats at the conference. Next, he characterized the bill he supported as the middle-of-the-road version. Senator Gaylord Nelson had proposed a bill to ban the internal combustion engine altogether, a ban that would have affected every car on the road at the time. Muskie informed the conference members that if they did not support the measures in the Senate Clean Air Act, they would be faced with Nelson's extreme bill. Furthermore, if they did not allow the bill to pass with the provision allowing citizens to sue, Senator Philip Hart, a liberal Democrat from Michigan, would push for an amendment to permit environmental class-action suits. In a class-action suit, lawyers claim to represent a class of people, a certain number of whom allege that they have been or will be harmed by a particular product or activity. Class-action suits frequently involve thousands of people, cost millions of dollars, and delay a business's or even an entire industry's operations for years. Conservatives, in particular, hated the idea of such suits. Muskie announced that senators would come back with a new bill the following year if the House did not agree to the Senate version.

Baker, who developed a reputation as "the great conciliator," contributed his skill to help win over the Republican members of the panel. A former senator, Fred Thompson, once described Baker's tactics: "His favorite approach is to say, 'That's a wonderful idea, and let me add to that, this,' and then come up with something that might be almost completely contrary to the original idea. But he presents it in a way that's building on, or cooperating with, or drawing on the best of more than one idea."

The strategy employed by Muskie and Baker worked. After twelve days of meetings, the conference members agreed to almost all of the Senate's provisions. The final agreement, announced on December 16, 1970, reduced spending for the bill from the Senate's proposed $1.19 billion over three years to $1.1 billion. The revised bill also reduced prison time for first-time pollution offenders from two years to one year. Penalties would be doubled for repeat offenders. Representative Rogers added a provision that required automakers to use the best technology developed by any inventor, not just by a company's own researchers, to meet air-quality standards. Deadlines on auto emissions, removal of lead from gasoline, and the submission and implementation of the states' own antipollution plans remained the same as those in the Senate bill. Both houses of Congress approved the agreement by voice vote shortly after the pact was announced.

"I don't think you'll find any place in American history, a bill that was as far reaching and with such scope as the Clean Air Act get enacted with such rapidity and with such unanimity," said Billings. "And that was because Muskie had a unique vision."

The Republican President Nixon, who had sided with the automakers in opposing the bill's deadlines on emissions, knew that if he vetoed the act, Congress would override his veto. If he took no action within ten days of the bill's passage and Congress was still in session, the legislation would automatically become law. However, if Congress had already adjourned before the ten days had passed, the president could take no action and the bill would die. This last strategy, known as a pocket veto, is one that presidents sometimes use to kill a bill that Congress passes late in a session and would otherwise enact by overriding a veto.

Despite rumors that he would employ a pocket veto, on December 31, 1970, two days before the ninety-first Congress adjourned, President Nixon signed the Clean Air Act into law (its official title is the National Air Quality Standards Act of 1970). He praised it as the most important clean-air bill yet and called 1970 the "year of the beginning" and 1971 the "year of action" regarding efforts to combat air pollution. Muskie, expected to run against Nixon for president in 1972, was not invited to the White House signing ceremony.

Representative Rogers called the legislation a "watershed that paved the way for the widespread consensus in our country . . . that air pollution control must be a top priority of the federal government." Senator John Sherman Cooper

President Richard M. Nixon signs the Clean Air Act in the White House in Washington, D.C., on December 31, 1970. William D. Ruckelshaus (*left*) director of the Environmental Protection Agency, and Russell Train, chairman of the Council on Environmental Quality, applaud the signing.

called the law "the most far-reaching piece of social legislation in American history." The act, according to Cooper, "would set in motion a course of events that history could not reverse." In Senator Howard Baker's view, the Clean Air Act was a "lasting legacy." He said his work on the bill was his proudest achievement. "In many respects," he declared, the act could "be said to have changed the world."

Muskie viewed the clean air campaign as a key element in winning the public's support in the fight against pollution in general. "Air pollution provided much of the momentum for our fight against all forms of pollution. You can escape water pollution . . . at least for a time," he wrote. "You cannot escape air pollution." According to Muskie, the law "began a

The Clean Air Act took aim at pollution such as the ash spewed by a coal-fueled power plant in New Johnsonville, Tennessee, pictured above on June 1, 1973.

process that yielded a change in the American people's fundamental relationship with their environment . . . and put in place an infrastructure of air quality planning and management throughout the country."

William D. Ruckelshaus became the first director of the EPA after the Senate approved his appointment on December 2. The agency's first order of business was to carry out the requirements of the Clean Air Act.

Clean Water Act of 1972

For years Congress had tried to control the industrial pollution of the nation's waterways. Efforts to pass legislation on oil spills stalled for more than a year when a joint conference failed to work out an agreement between a tougher Senate bill and a weaker House version. Senator Edmund Muskie, taking his usual legislative approach, decided to wait rather than give in. As it had in the past, Muskie's patience paid off.

During the next session, Congress passed the Water Quality Improvement Act of 1970, which had even tougher standards than the 1968 version of the law. Muskie and Howard Baker of Tennessee worked together to write a law that would make those responsible for oil spills pay the cleanup costs. This provision laid the basis for the Superfund legislation—requiring polluters of all kinds to help pay for cleanup—that came a decade later.

President Richard Nixon supported the House bill, which

made a shipowner liable for a spill only when it could be proven that the spill was not a mishap but a willful or negligent action. Muskie's Senate version made shipowners responsible even when spills occurred accidentally.

In February 1970 a major oil spill in Tampa Bay helped change a key vote on the bill. The spill emptied 10,000 gallons of oil into the ocean waters off western Florida. The Humble Oil Company owned the grounded tanker that had carried the oil. Representative William C. Cramer of Florida, the ranking Republican on the House Committee on Public Works, had resisted efforts to make the House bill's provisions more stringent. After the oil spill in his home district, however, Cramer reversed his position and criticized the owner's handling of the spill: "It's an outrage, it's a disgrace, it's absolutely inadequate."

With Cramer's vote, the Senate version of the bill won the support of the joint conference and of Congress. The new law, signed by President Nixon on April 3, 1970, required shipowners to pay up to $14 million or $100 a gross ton (whichever was less) to clean up oil spills. Owners of facilities on land had to pay up to $8 million to clean up oil discharges from their plants. Owners were liable unless the pollution resulted from an act of God, war, or the negligence of the U.S. government or another party.

A BILL TO CLEAN AMERICA'S WATERS

Compared with water pollution, oil pollution proved to be just a drop in the bucket. Federal money had helped small cities and towns build federally mandated sewage treatment plants, but bigger cities needed larger and more advanced systems to treat their wastes. Of the $3.4 billion authorized by the Clean Water Restoration Act of 1966, only

People lounge and play on the beach and in the waters of Lake Erie at Sterling State Park, near Monroe, Michigan, in 1968 despite a sign warning of pollution.

$2.2 billion had been released by Presidents Johnson and Nixon. With industrial wastes also continuing to flow into America's waterways, by the early 1970s only slightly more than a third of the nation's rivers, lakes, and streams were safe enough to swim or fish in.

Several congressmen and President Nixon turned to the 1899 Refuse Act to tighten regulations on industrial dumping. In December 1970 Nixon issued an executive order, based on the old law, that required federal permits before companies could discharge wastes into rivers and streams. States would have a say in issuing the permits for the waterways within their borders. The order also gave the EPA the go-ahead on developing national standards for discharges. Environmentalists criticized the order, however, because it gave power to states, which had, they claimed, for years allowed the fouling of rivers and streams.

Early in 1971 both Nixon and Muskie proposed bills to expand the Federal Water Pollution Control Act. Muskie introduced his bill in the Senate on February 2. While the bill ostensibly amended the earlier clean-water law, it really offered radically different solutions to the water-pollution problem. The bill, which became known as the Clean Water Act, adopted many of the strategies of the Clean Air Act. It set strict water-quality goals and deadlines and called for national water standards. Under the Muskie bill, states would be given three months to adopt the water standards and develop a water-quality program and three years to meet EPA standards. Those discharging anything into waterways were required to get permits to do so. The EPA could veto permits issued by a state if the state did not meet federal water-quality standards.

As in the air-pollution bill, Muskie relied on yet-to-occur advances in technology to accomplish his goals. "What we think we can do is not enough," Muskie noted. New plants and facilities would be required to install systems that would remove pollutants from wastewater and allow the water to be recycled. The bill also called for $25 billion over five years for antipollution projects and gave the EPA regulatory power over all U.S. waters, not just those that involved more than one state. The bill's declared aim was to make all U.S. waters clean enough for swimming and fishing within ten years. The measure also set a goal of eliminating polluted discharges into U.S. waters by 1985.

The legislation represented a major change in how the government dealt with water pollution. In the past, industries and municipalities could dump wastes into rivers and streams as long as the discharge did not worsen the overall quality of the water. Under that system, industries might

Piles of garbage washed ashore by rising tides litter the shores of Tangier Island, Virginia, in 1971.

continue dumping into already polluted rivers and streams. The Muskie bill's aim was the total elimination of polluting discharges. Discharges were to meet given standards *before* being dumped. Industries were to adopt the "best practicable" antipollution technology by 1976 and the "best available" technology by 1981.

Nixon's proposal also called for federal water-quality standards and required permits for all discharges. Both bills barred discharges that did not meet the standards. Both also prohibited discharges that would lower the quality of waters that were cleaner than federal standards required. Unlike the Muskie bill, Nixon's proposals did not include a ban on polluting discharges for all new facilities and did not set deadlines for meeting water-quality standards.

The Nixon proposals, presented on February 10 to Congress, contained seven words that made it much more appealing to industry than the Muskie bill. The words, "taking into account the practicality of compliance," offered companies a loophole that environmentalists believed would considerably weaken attempts to enforce the bill. Such language left it up to company officials, government bureaucrats, and, in disputed cases, judges to decide whether federal water standards were practical. Representatives of industry had already protested to the administration that the proposed clean-air and clean-water standards would cost companies an excessive amount and moreover could not be met using available technology.

The Senate turned the Muskie bill over to the Subcommittee on Air and Water Pollution (still chaired by Muskie) for review. While the subcommittee considered the bill, Muskie ran an unsuccessful campaign for president. In his absence, Senator Thomas Eagleton temporarily chaired the subcommittee. Muskie kept in close contact with the subcommittee from the campaign trail and returned to Washington often to participate in the hearings. He waited out his opponents until he finally got most of what he wanted.

James Buckley, a member of the Conservative Party from New York, joined the subcommittee in 1971. Muskie made a point of listening to, and considering, his ideas. As a conservative, Buckley opposed federal regulation on principle. Nevertheless, he became convinced that air and water pollution had to be handled at a national level. Conservatives, he said, needed to be educated about the seriousness of the pollution problem. They had not "sufficiently awakened to a totally new phenomenon, namely that we are injecting into water and air huge quantities of totally artificial chemicals that didn't exist until after World War II." Buckley later helped lead the floor fight for the Clean Water Act.

Several conservative Republicans and some Democrats, however, joined business groups in opposing the bill. Their arguments focused on three major points:

- States, not the federal government, should have power to control waterways within their borders.
- The bill's price tag would cost businesses and taxpayers too much.
- Companies could not meet the deadlines for waste treatment because of the high cost and the lack of technological solutions.

Lobbyists for industry tried to stall the bill. A spokesman for the U.S. Chamber of Commerce, representing businesses across the country, predicted that overly strict air and water regulations would force whole industries to close their doors. In testimony before Muskie's subcommittee in May, the spokesman warned that government would have to deal with the chaos if businesses shut down because they could not afford to pay for antipollution measures required by the new laws or if technology did not advance fast enough to allow them to comply.

Surprisingly, two Nixon administration sources provided information that tended to support stringent regulation. The annual report of the White House Council on Environmental Quality, issued in August, contradicted the business group's pessimistic predictions. The council reported that pollution-control efforts, while costly, would be "well within the capacity of the American economy to absorb." Antipollution measures would cost billions, the report acknowledged, but it noted that pollution cost even more in damage to the environment and health. President Nixon, however, expressed reservations about the cost of controlling pollution. Many conservative Republicans and business interests continued to urge the president to ease environmental regulations.

In May 1971 the head of the U.S. Government Accountability Office (GAO) told Congress that current laws on water pollution were "slow and cumbersome." Testifying before the House Public Works Committee, GAO Comptroller General Elmer B. Staats called for changes to allow the EPA to take quicker action. Under the 1965 Federal Water Pollution Control Act, the EPA had to get the approval of a state's governor before acting in that state. When pollution affected more than one state, the EPA could act on its own, but the process took "a minimum of 58 weeks" to get to court, Staats said. "The EPA can act under present law only after water pollution is already a problem," he said. He asked Congress for a law that would set standards to control discharges into rivers, streams, and ocean waters. He also expressed the opinion that industries were not paying a fair share of the costs.

Muskie's subcommittee held hearings for thirty-three days and spent weeks more marking up the bill, revising it, and preparing it for a vote by the full Senate. On November 2, 1971, the Senate voted 86 to 0 with fourteen absentees to approve the Clean Water Act. The final version authorized $20 billion over four years for pollution control, including $14 billion for sewage-treatment plants.

Meanwhile, the House considered the version backed by President Nixon. Nixon, who took a more conservative approach to cleaning up the environment, preferred less aggressive enforcement and opposed a 1985 deadline for an end to discharging pollutants. Nixon's version also reduced the federal funds allotted for municipal sewage-treatment plants to $6 billion over three years.

Several Democrats proposed amendments to the bill, which they considered too weak. Environmentalists, public-interest groups, and labor unions pushed for these more stringent provisions. The amendments, however, met strong opposition during a round of public hearings held at the president's request. Members of the administration, including the EPA director, joined industry representatives in opposing the amendments. In January 1972 the chairman of Allied Chemical Corporation urged Congress not to vote on a bill that, he said, would damage the nation's economy.

The House rejected the amendments and passed a version of the Nixon bill on March 29, 1972, on a 378 to 14 vote. This version set aside $24.6 billion over three years to deal with dirty water. Yet it included $18.3 billion for treatment plants, more than in the Senate bill and four times the amount proposed by the president. It cut a provision that allowed citizens to file suit to enforce the law. The House bill granted industries a two-year delay in adopting new antipollution technology if the EPA ruled it an economic hardship.

In addition, the House gave states sole authority to issue discharge permits. Only when discharges affected other states could the EPA veto a permit. In addition, the House measure allowed industries in some cases to dilute rather than treat polluted water before its discharge into a waterway, nor did it require industries to get a permit to discharge wastes into public sewers. After the vote, Muskie told the press, "A massive White House lobbying effort on behalf of special interests has succeeded in defeating these vital amendments." So great were the differences between the Senate and House versions, in fact, that political analysts predicted that Congress would not pass a clean-water bill during that session. They overlooked Muskie's tenacity and his commitment to clean water.

A "GIANT STEP" TOWARD CLEAN WATER

In April 1972, four months after declaring his candidacy for president, Muskie withdrew from active campaigning. His public support had begun to wane after he defended his wife from charges raised against her in New Hampshire's *Union Leader* newspaper. Some observers said Muskie had cried during the incident; he himself contended that falling snowflakes had wet his cheeks. In July Democrats chose Senator George McGovern as their candidate for president. McGovern selected Thomas Eagleton, who had chaired the Senate Subcommittee on Air and Water Pollution during Muskie's absence, as his vice presidential running mate. Eagleton, too, later dropped out over questions about his treatment for depression, a matter he had failed to disclose to McGovern. Eagleton was replaced by Sargent Shriver.

After the unsuccessful presidential campaign, Muskie returned to the Senate determined to win passage of an acceptable Clean Water Act. On May 11 and for the next four months, members of the House and the Senate met to hammer out a compromise bill, one that both houses could support. By mid-August the only unresolved issue involved hot water. The Senate's version required that heated water be regulated, just as other discharges would be, while the House's provided a loophole that allowed the EPA to exempt industries discharging hot water if the economic and social costs greatly outweighed the benefits of antipollution measures. The National Association of Electric Companies, whose members discharged huge amounts of hot water, provided the wording in the House bill, according to congressional insiders. The Senate bill's proponents, noting that hot-water discharges killed various forms of plant and animal marine life, argued that one segment of industry should not be given preferential treatment. Conference members eventually agreed to treat hot water as a pollutant. Restrictions might be eased, however, if a factory owner who released heated water could prove that the discharge did not endanger plant and animal life in the affected waterway.

On September 14, 1972, after thirty-nine meetings, the conference members unanimously approved a compromise bill. The final bill, much more restrictive than the House version, delayed some deadlines but contained most of the requirements desired by the Senate. It set two goals: to make America's rivers and streams clean enough for swimming and fishing within ten years and to eliminate the discharge of pollutants into America's waterways by the year 1985.

To accomplish these goals, the bill included provisions that:

- Called for national water-quality standards to be established by the EPA.
- Barred industries and municipalities from dumping untreated wastes in U.S. waters and required EPA-approved permits for treated discharges.
- Gave industries until July 1, 1977, to control pollution using the best practicable technology (an additional year over the Senate version) and until 1983 to put in place the best available technology (an extra two years).
- Allotted $24.6 billion over a three-year period for sewage-treatment plants and research into water pollution. The amount was four times more

than Nixon had proposed. With federal grants to municipalities covering 75 percent of the cost of building new treatment plants, poorer states that had not been able to afford previous government antipollution programs, could participate.

- Authorized $2.75 billion to reimburse municipalities for antipollution projects already under way.
- Allowed states to issue discharge permits to industries and municipalities; the EPA would have the power to issue permits in states that failed to meet water-quality standards.
- Required permits to dredge, fill, or drain wetlands. The EPA and the U.S. Army Corps of Engineers shared jurisdiction over wetlands, with the EPA having final say over permits.
- Gave citizens the right to sue the EPA, the states, and polluters over water pollution issues.

On October 4, Senator Muskie introduced the conference bill to the Senate. He portrayed it as a matter of life and death for the nation. The legislation, he said, addressed the "cancer of water pollution" that "threatens our very existence and which will not respond to the kind of treatment that has been prescribed in the past." The measure would mandate that pollutants be treated at the source, and every community would be required to install advanced systems to treat wastes. Only by getting billions of dollars of federally provided funds could municipalities afford to build such treatment plants, Muskie said. He also noted that the necessary advances in technology would not occur without even more federal money and a larger federal commitment.

Senator Jennings Randolph, a Democrat from West Virginia

and chairman of the Committee on Public Works, said the bill would speed the cleanup of America's rivers and streams and help communities and states do their part in fighting pollution. Even though the bill carried a big price tag, he said, it would "pay great and lasting dividends," which would "be willingly borne by the American people." Other senators of both parties took their turn in praising the bill. Senator John Sherman Cooper, a Republican member of Muskie's subcommittee, called the bill "one of the most significant, most comprehensive, most thoroughly debated pieces of environmental legislation ever to be considered by the Congress." Later that day the Senate voted unanimously, 74 to 0, to pass the Clean Water Act of 1972.

The House, in a similar response, approved it 366 to 11. Representative Robert E. Jones Jr., a Democrat from Alabama who had served on the House-Senate conference committee, asked his fellow House members to pass the bill with a "margin so overwhelming" that it would show that "Congress has the will and the leadership to save our priceless waters from the degradation that is fast destroying them." As in the Senate, both Democrats and Republicans in the House spoke in favor of the bill.

OVERRIDING A VETO

The power to enact the bill into law fell to President Richard Nixon. By law, the president had until midnight on October 17 to take action. If Congress had already adjourned by then, as originally planned, the president could use a pocket veto to kill the bill. To prevent that from happening, Democratic leaders let it be known that Congress would stay in session until after the deadline. Republicans in both the House and the Senate urged the president to sign the bill to allow

Congress to adjourn on time. Senators and House members were eager to get back to their districts and campaign for voter support in the upcoming elections.

The EPA's administrator, William Ruckelshaus, reversing his earlier stand, recommended that Nixon sign the bill. "It seems reasonable to me to spend less than 1 percent of the Federal budget and two-tenths of 1 percent of the gross national product over the next several years to assure for future generations the very survival of the gross national product," he wrote in a thirty-three-page memo.

Ruckelshaus's plea failed to sway the president. On October 17 President Nixon, no longer pressured by Muskie's campaign as the environmental candidate, vetoed the Clean Water Act. He said in a statement issued shortly before midnight that he opposed the bill because of his concerns that the "budget-wrecking" legislation would lead to "spiraling prices and increasingly onerous taxes." Citing his own support of environmental protection, Nixon nevertheless said that improving water quality by "extreme and needless overspending" did not serve the public's interest. Senator McGovern, the Democratic presidential candidate, criticized the veto as a "mean-spirited action by a President who has always put special interests before the public interest."

Congress wasted little time responding to the veto. In the early morning hours of October 18, the Senate met to consider the issue. After rejecting Nixon's claims that the bill would break the budget, Muskie again raised the questions he had posed earlier, when the Senate voted on the conference bill. "Can we afford clean water?" he asked. "Can we afford rivers and lakes and streams and oceans which continue to make life possible on this planet? Can we afford life itself? . . . These questions answer themselves." Shortly after

Stinky Sludge to Clean Water

In addition to promoting the Clean Air and Clean Water acts in Congress, Edmund Muskie also had to convince voters back in Maine that his actions would benefit them. During his 1976 campaign for reelection to the Senate, he stopped at a paper mill in Westbrook. Meeting with the candidate in the firm's conference room, the company's executives bluntly told Muskie that the Clean Air Act and Clean Water Act regulations had cost them a lot of money and had harmed their business.

"How many machines were you running in the 1960s?" he asked the officials. They told him. "And how many machines are you operating now?" he asked. The figure was about double that of the previous decade.

"You know," he said in his slow nasal twang, "I don't think I hurt you that much if you have that many machines going." Turning his head, he gazed thoughtfully out the window at the Presumpscot River, which had once been one of the dirtiest bodies of water in the state, a "stinky, slow-moving sludge," according to a fisherman who played along its banks as a child.

"And this river," Muskie noted, nodding at the flowing water below, "is much cleaner now than it was then."

Whatever they may have been thinking, the company officials had nothing more to say.

1 a.m. on October 18, 1972, the Senate voted 52 to 12 to override President Nixon's veto. Later in the day, when the House voted 247 to 23 in favor of the bill, Congress overrode the veto and the Clean Water Act of 1972 became law.

Many members had already left Washington to campaign for their seats in an election less than three weeks away. Among those remaining, Republicans joined Democrats in support of the veto override. Although Senator James Buckley expressed sympathy for Nixon's desire to reduce costs, he joined the majority. "I feel we are simply beyond the point where we can afford further delays," he told fellow senators, "and by 'afford' I speak in terms of [both] environmental and economic costs."

Other Republicans either voting for or supporting an override included the House Minority Leader, Gerald R. Ford, and Senator Howard Baker. The Clean Water Act, Baker said, was "far and away the most significant and promising piece of environmental legislation ever enacted by Congress."

In 2008, thirty-six years after the enactment of the Clean Water Act of 1972, the chairman of the House Committee on Transportation and Infrastructure noted that since the legislation's passage, the number of rivers and streams safe for swimming, fishing, and drinking had doubled. "The Clean Water Act," said Representative James L. Oberstar, a Democrat from Minnesota, "has singlehandedly taken us from the days where the Cuyahoga River caught fire and Lake Erie was pronounced 'dead' to the days where two-thirds of assessed rivers and streams meet 'fishable and swimmable' standards." The act, he added, is considered by industry, environmentalists, Republicans, and Democrats "one of the most important environmental statutes ever enacted."

CHAPTER SEVEN

The Campaign Continues

Shortly after Richard Nixon's reelection as president in November 1972, he began seeking ways to limit congressionally approved spending, particularly for the Clean Water Act. Of the federal funds allotted to states and municipalities in fiscal year 1973 for the construction of sewage-treatment plants, the president ordered the head of the Environmental Protection Agency to release no more than $2 billion, only 40 percent of the funds Congress had pledged in the Clean Water Act. In the following year, states were to receive only $3 billion, 50 percent of the money allotted.

For years presidents had used this strategy to curtail congressional spending. This time New York City, other municipalities, and several states sued the EPA to compel release of the federal antipollution funds due them. By the time the Supreme Court heard the case, Russell E. Train was EPA administrator, and so the case became known as *Train* v. *City of New York*. On February 18, 1975, the Court, unanimously deciding in favor of the cities and states, ruled that the Clean Water Act did not allow the president to withhold the money and ordered the EPA to release it to qualifying entities.

NEW INITIATIVES IN THE 1970S

As a result of the Clean Air Act, researchers developed new devices, called catalytic converters, which reduced auto emissions. While air quality in many cities did not improve, at least it did not deteriorate. In some areas the air did get better. Critics—and even some who worked for passage of the legislation—said the act set itself an impossibly high goal. Ironically, its toughness weakened it and made it difficult to enforce. When industry and municipalities were unable to meet the deadlines, Congress was forced to extend them. The growing sense that the act's standards and deadlines were unreasonable left them open to legal attack. As industries and cities and towns sought judicial relief, activist citizen groups sued to force compliance.

Muskie, later admitting that he and his colleagues had pushed through the law while public enthusiasm ran high, said, "We set goals, standards, and objectives beyond our reach." He said that the law's supporters regarded the act not as "the ultimate solution" but as "pioneering legislation" that redefined government's role in protecting the public.

In 1975 Muskie's subcommittee began consideration of a bill to "fine-tune" the original Clean Air Act. After industry missed several deadlines, Congress considered reviewing the law's effectiveness and its progress in reducing air pollution. By that time, however, American industries were better prepared to contest new regulations. With gasoline shortages and inflation threatening the economy and the entire American way of life, the public's concern shifted to fuel-efficient and less expensive automobiles. It was widely believed that antipollution devices raised car prices and reduced gas mileage, but Muskie contended that the size of automobiles and engines affected fuel efficiency more than the devices did.

Under the 1970 law's standards, carmakers were supposed to install new pollution-control devices to reduce hydrocarbon, carbon monoxide, and nitrogen oxide emissions by 1977—that is, in their 1978 models. The carmakers called the deadline unmeetable. Similarly, electric companies, steel manufacturers, coal plants, and others balked at the expense of installing high-tech "scrubbers" that were designed to remove sulfur-laden gases from emissions. Theoretically, the scrubbers would control pollution at the source, before it escaped into the air. The companies preferred a less expensive method: testing air quality and shutting down when pollution got too bad. Industry representatives, pointing out that scrubber technology would improve in the future, argued that Congress should postpone its mandates until better equipment came along.

Muskie contended that better devices would come along much more quickly if the law imposed deadlines. Firms would be forced to invest in research to comply with air-quality standards. If industry were allowed to wait for better technology, air quality would get worse, and the public's health would be endangered. "Certainly, knowledge is incomplete," Muskie told representatives of an electric company in 1975. "But at some point we've got to take some risks, and the question is whether we err on the side of public health or err on the side of what someone says is cost-effective." The senator also expressed his belief that if companies did not now adopt the best measures available, any future solution would be even more costly.

Congress worked to amend the Clean Air Act for almost two years. In the fall of 1976 the House-Senate conference agreed on a compromise bill, which included the Senate's demanding air-quality standards but gave automakers an extra year to meet them. Carmakers still opposed the bill, as did other industries affected by the requirements. Senator Jake Garn, a Utah Republican who opposed a section that limited development in areas with air cleaner than the standards required, led a filibuster that blocked Senate action on the bill. When Congress adjourned before a vote could be taken, the bill died. Muskie acknowledged defeat but continued his campaign in the next Congress.

An amending bill that finally passed in August 1977 gave automakers until the 1980 model year to incorporate antipollution devices in their cars. They had threatened to shut down their assembly lines if Congress required them to install the devices in the 1978 models. Though the new law also gave states more time, in some cases up to ten years, to develop antipollution programs, it also included a measure that affected areas of the country with minimal pollution. New industries could open in those areas only if operations did not significantly worsen air quality.

In December 1977, after another two-year battle, Congress also amended the Clean Water Act. The amending measure included $24.5 billion for municipal sewage-treatment plants and $4.2 billion more for research and related costs. As with the clean-air amendments, the clean-water revisions extended the original act's deadlines and allowed extensions for industries, cities, and towns on a case-by-case basis. The new provisions gave the EPA authority to crack down on those who dumped toxic chemicals into U.S. waters and made shipowners liable for oil spills that occurred within two hundred miles of U.S. shores, a huge extension of the original act's twelve-mile limit.

The amended law's most controversial measures affected wetlands. The final bill put the Army Corps of Engineers in charge of issuing permits for wetlands dredging, filling, and other activities but gave the EPA the right to veto unacceptable projects. Normal farming and forestry activities did not require permits. States won the right, with EPA approval, to set up their own programs to protect wetlands. As part of the House-Senate compromise, federal projects authorized by Congress that required wetlands dredging were exempted from EPA regulations. Environmentalists objected to this last provision.

THE SECOND DECADE

In 1980, ten years after the Clean Air Act and eight years after the Clean Water Act became law, the nation had made significant gains. Air quality had improved dramatically ("the decade's success story," wrote the *New York Times*). Twenty-five major cities had far fewer "unhealthful" days, marked by heavy concentrations of air pollution. New York and Los Angeles, however, continued to log unhealthily dirty air two days out of every three.

Gains attributable to the Clean Water Act were less dramatic. Water quality had improved in 1972 and at least had not gotten worse since then, the President's Council on Environmental Quality reported. The lack of further gains was partly related to the impact of storm runoff and groundwater, which were not regulated by the Clean Water Act, on rivers and streams.

The best news for environmentalists was the increased awareness of pollution and voters' continuing support for measures to combat it. "Ten years ago there were only a handful of adults in this country who knew what the word 'ecology' meant," said Douglas M. Costle, EPA's administrator. "Today every schoolchild is taught ecology. Environmental protection is becoming a permanent part of our political value system."

In 1980, looking back on environmental progress in the 1970s, Muskie insisted on the need to continue the battle. "Every new proposal must be backed by the most persuasive and understandable arguments," he said. Claiming that businesses, not having the public welfare as their primary goal, would balk at new laws requiring them to spend money on cleaning up pollution, he said that "environmental progress" would be accomplished not only by new laws but by "a fresh enthusiasm for the old ones."

He also cautioned against turning environmentalism into an elitist cause. "It will not be enough to save a wilderness for a few hundred canoeists with the time and money to enjoy it," he said. The environment's champions had to make the movement "more relevant to the lives of more Americans" by coming up with alternatives to oil that were "acceptable, available, and affordable" and by accommodating America's "dream of opportunity." Otherwise, environmental legislation could collapse under pressure from those who placed jobs, energy, and other matters ahead of antipollution measures.

As Muskie had predicted, President Ronald Reagan's administration (1981–1989) tried to dismantle the antipollution legislation that others had enacted. The Republican Reagan pledged during the 1980 presidential campaign to ease environmental restrictions on business. Shortly after his election but before he assumed office, Republicans in Congress joined with Democrats to pass the Superfund law (the Comprehensive Environmental Response, Compensation, and Liability Act), which required those responsible for depositing hazardous wastes in landfills to pay for the cleanup.

Despite this show of support for environmental issues by the outgoing Congress, Reagan proposed major cuts in environmental programs and the EPA's budget, most of which the new Congress rejected, along with administration proposals permitting an increase in oil drilling and coal operations. Several Reagan appointees—notably James Watt, the secretary of the interior, and Anne Gorsuch, the EPA director—openly criticized environmental laws, declined to enforce them, and tried to weaken the Clean Air and Clean Water acts. Congress held hearings into the EPA's failure to manage the Superfund. The EPA's director of the program went to jail after lying under oath during the hearings, and Gorsuch was forced to resign because of misconduct at the EPA under her watch. Watt was fired after a remark about a coal-advisory panel created an uproar in the press. A reinvigorated environmental movement ultimately won support for even more controversial legislation.

A heavily Democratic Congress easily overrode Reagan's veto of the Water Quality Act of 1987. The law reauthorized the 1972 Clean Water Act and added regulations to control storm-water runoff and toxic hot spots (concentrations of heavy metals and chemicals in the water).

CLEAN AIR ACT AMENDMENTS OF 1990

By 1990 the Clean Air Act required another major overhaul. While some air pollutants had decreased significantly, the earth's climate had become warmer, a condition that most scientists predicted could lead to weather-related disasters.

This condition, called global warming or the greenhouse effect, has been tied to the atmospheric buildup of carbon dioxide, once thought harmless, and other gases, mainly from emissions from cars, power plants, and fuels such as coal and oil. These "greenhouse gases" cover the earth and trap heat from the sun. These and certain other gases also form acid rain, which is especially harmful to plants and aquatic animals. Other gases have damaged the layer of ozone that protects the earth from the sun's rays.

"The concept of 'solving' environmental problems is far more complex than we ever anticipated," said Malcolm Murray, a professor of environmental law and former assistant director of natural resources in Colorado. "We didn't expect the advent of new problems—the ozone layer, global warming, acid rain—and they are the gravest threats to human survival. It's not good guy, bad guy . . . the fixes are not that quick."

Reagan's successor, George H. W. Bush, billing himself the "environmental president," supported Clean Air Act amendments in 1990 that aimed at controlling smog, acid rain, and toxic particles in the air. The 1990 law also required auto manufacturers to install devices on new cars that would reduce carbon monoxide, hydrocarbons, and nitrogen oxide to a much greater degree.

An innovation introduced by the 1990 amendments involved a trading system that allowed the buying and selling of "emission allotments." Under the system, dubbed cap and trade, the government placed a cap on the total emissions allowed an industry, with each company allotted a percentage of the emissions. Companies that had low emissions could sell their allotment to firms that required more than their initial share. The idea was to give the industry some flexibility and spur companies to cut costs by reducing emissions. Over the next

In a ceremony in the East Room of the White House, President George H. W. Bush signs the Clean Air Act amendments on November 16, 1990, as EPA administrator William Reilly (*left*) and Energy secretary James Watkins (*right*) look on.

fifteen years, sulfur dioxide emissions fell by five million tons, and those of nitrogen oxide by three million.

With the passage of the 1990 amendments, American business began resigning itself to antipollution measures. A lobbyist representing more than two thousand businesses reflected that industrial leaders had come to accept clean air and water regulations as "part of the cost of doing business." Professor Murray agreed that environmental requirements were no longer automatically greeted with hostility. "Some of our major progress is the voluntary acceptance of industry to do things that in the past might have taken regulation. . . . In part it's because people reaching middle and upper management today grew up with that environmental awareness."

SETBACKS

Despite changes in attitude, the Clean Water Act has never lacked for opponents intent on weakening or eliminating its provisions. The House voted in 1995 to relax many of the regulations in the act, but the Senate fought back the attempt. Had the bill passed, states would have regained more control over environmental regulations within their borders, and federal officials would have had to give more consideration to the costs associated with water-quality standards. The bill also would have ended the EPA's authority to override Army Corps of Engineers' decisions. President Bill Clinton called the legislation "the Dirty Water Bill."

The goal of clean water remained elusive thirty years after passage of the Clean Water Act. In 2000, the EPA reported that 40 percent of the nation's waterways still were not clean enough for fishing and swimming. Environmental groups blamed lack of enforcement. "The U.S. EPA has lost control of environmental law enforcement and, in the absence of strong federal oversight, many states have gutted environmental enforcement programs," the Environmental Working Group reported in 2000.

In 2001 and 2006, the Supreme Court dealt damaging blows to the Clean Water Act by ending its protection of wetlands and small ponds and streams. A 2001 decision involving a dispute between an Illinois solid-waste agency and the Corps of Engineers removed waters not considered navigable from the reach of the act. The ruling returned to state and local authorities the power to regulate small ponds and other waters not suitable for navigation within their borders.

In two 2006 cases the Supreme Court ruled that the Clean Water Act did not cover wetlands. The cases, *Rapanos* v. *United States* and *Carabell* v. *United States Army Corps of Engineers*, led to a 5 to 4 decision allowing developers to fill in wetlands to build a shopping mall and a condominium complex in Michigan. The wetlands, while unnavigable, drained into a river in one case and a lake in the other.

EPA officials estimated that the rulings affected some 20 million acres of wetlands and 60 percent of U.S. streams, but no one knew for sure exactly which bodies of water were involved. Environmental experts predicted that if wetlands and small streams became polluted, the dirty water would flow to larger rivers and lakes and contaminate them. Since 2001 more than 10,000 wetlands, streams, ponds, and other bodies of water have been filled or polluted without federal intervention, according to an environmental group called Earth Justice.

GLOBAL WARMING AND OTHER CHALLENGES

Since passage of the original Clean Air Act in 1970, cleaner diesel fuels and engines are in use, lead-free gasoline has become the norm, and power plants and manufacturing facilities have significantly cut their emissions. Nevertheless, a study conducted by the American Lung Association in 2010 showed that more than half of Americans still breathed air dangerously contaminated by either ozone or soot. The number of motor vehicles on the road continues to climb, increasing the amount of toxic emissions in the air and adding to global warming.

The Kyoto Treaty, which had been ratified by 187 nations as of October 2009, was aimed at reducing six gases linked to global warming. Countries ratifying the treaty, which went into effect in 2005, agreed to abide by its limits on emissions of these gases. The United States signed the plan but did not ratify the treaty. In 2001 President George W. Bush withdrew U.S. support for the treaty. He and others who opposed the treaty contended that it would harm the U.S. economy.

President Bush again cited economic reasons when he pushed for oil and gas exploration in protected national forests and for oil drilling in Alaska's wilderness. Extracting Alaskan oil and gas would help free the nation from its dependence on foreign sources of fuel, he said. Environmental groups challenged the proposal in court, and it was set aside after Bush left office in January 2009.

The Court came down on the side of the Clean Air Act in two rulings issued in 2007. In the first, in *Massachusetts* v. *Environmental Protection Agency*, the Court sided with Massachusetts in ruling that the EPA had the authority to regulate carbon dioxide and other gases blamed for global warming. The Bush administration had argued that the Clean Air Act did not cover such gases. The second ruling, in *Environmental Defense et al.* v. *Duke Energy Corp.*, confirmed EPA's right to require factories and power plants to update their anti-pollution systems when they expanded or renovated.

The Bush administration took other actions that angered environmentalists. The EPA denied California's request in 2007 to set auto-emissions standards that were more stringent than those required by federal guidelines. In the waning days of his presidency, President Bush issued more than 150 regulations, among them some that eased Clean Air and Clean Water Act regulations. The new rules:

- Lifted the ban on coal-fired plants near national parks and similar areas with little pollution.
- Eased rules that required utility companies to upgrade antipollution systems when expanding or renovating their plants.
- Barred regulation of greenhouse gas emissions from oil refineries.

- Permitted farmers to avoid Clean Water Act procedures as long as they said they were not dumping animal wastes into rivers and streams.
- Allowed mining companies to dump toxic wastes in valleys and streams.

NEW EFFORTS

Environmentalists were cheered at the election in 2008 of Barack Obama, an Illinois Democrat, as president and of a Democrat-controlled Congress. They hoped the new political climate would support environmental issues and result in the passage of amendments to the Clean Air and Clean Water acts. Shortly after taking office in January 2009, President Obama blocked enforcement of two air-quality rules issued by his predecessor, one of which would have allowed oil refineries to emit greenhouse gases (gases that are said to contribute to global warming). The EPA's new chief, Lisa Jackson, ordered coal-mining companies to stop dumping waste into Appalachian valleys and streams. Other regulations already in force, however, remained in place.

In April 2009 the EPA issued a finding that greenhouse gases were a threat to public health and welfare. The finding, in part a response to the Supreme Court decision on the matter, was a prelude to the EPA's regulation of the gases and its active involvement in the global warming issue.

In May 2009, after approving California's request to require auto-emissions standards more stringent than the EPA's, Obama issued revised mileage and emissions standards agreeable to both automobile makers and environmentalists. The standards required new cars to average 35.5 miles per gallon and to reduce greenhouse gases in their emissions by almost a third by 2016. This order marked the first time that federal regulation had been imposed on greenhouse gases emitted by automobiles. The order presented automakers with one national standard, which they had asked for, and matched the standard adopted by California.

"This is the single biggest step the American government has ever taken to cut greenhouse gas emissions," said Daniel Becker of Safe Climate Campaign, a consumer advocacy group in Washington, D.C. The *New York Times* lauded the move as "a huge step forward."

In December 2009 the United States participated in a United Nations conference dealing with global warming. Joining other industrialized nations, the United States pledged to reduce greenhouse-gas emissions by 2020. In contrast, however, in July 2010 the Senate rejected an Obama-backed energy bill aimed at capping U.S. emissions ahead of the UN's target year. The president said he intended "to keep pushing for broader reform, including climate legislation."

WHEN THERE IS NO ONE SOURCE

The nature of environmental problems has changed little from Senator Muskie's day to the second decade of the twenty-first century. Dirty air and dirty water still do not stay within one state's boundaries. The poorest states still tend to see stringent regulation as a threat to jobs and economic prosperity and so take a lenient approach to enforcement. Yet each state's actions affect not only its own citizens but all those who live downstream or downwind.

The Clean Water Act has had the most success in limiting pollution created at specific factories and sewage-treatment plants—so-called point-source pollution. But pollution from runoff —water that flows or seeps from the land to the shore and from contaminated groundwater and other nonspecific sources—remains under state government control and continues to pose problems.

Regulatory efforts to clean the air face similar problems. Individual states have little say over pollutants that originate elsewhere, unless the Clean Air Act specifically covers them. Northeastern states have been at the end of the nation's "tailpipe"—where pollutants from midwestern smokestacks accumulate. A number of politicians from these states want federal regulatory standards for emissions.

The EPA has drawn up rules to control both air and water pollution, but courts have overturned some EPA regulations and delayed others. The Supreme Court's ruling in 2006 that the Clean Water Act covers only navigable waters, for example, limited EPA's ability to enforce regulations in certain areas. Some developers have even contested the need to apply for permits for projects near waterways under question. Since the Court in 2006 did not specify exactly which waterways were covered by the law, the EPA has shut down or delayed action in more than 1,500 cases.

"We are in essence shutting down our Clean Water programs in some states," Douglas F. Mundrick, an EPA lawyer, told the *New York Times*. New York's drinking water comes from many sources that will no longer be protected by the Clean Water Act because of the Court ruling, said James Tierney, the state's assistant commissioner for water resources. "We need something to fix these gaps," Tierney said. "The Clean Water Act worked for over 30 years, and we're at risk of losing that if we can't get a new law."

Others, however, believe the Court's decisions have helped rein in a federal agency with too much power. The Congress that passed the original Clean Water Act "did not intend it to be unlimited" in its ability to regulate the nation's waterways, said Don Parrish. As a representative of the American Farm Bureau Federation, Parrish has opposed making changes in the law.

NEW BILLS INTRODUCED

Beginning in 2002, lawmakers introduced bills in each Congress to counteract the limits placed in 2001 (then again in 2006) on the Clean Water Act by the Supreme Court. The 2007 version of the Clean Water Restoration Act, introduced several times by Representative James Oberstar, attracted 176 cosponsors, mostly Democrats but a handful of Republicans, too. The measure removed the Court's exemption of "nonnavigable" waters under the Clean Water Act. The Senate considered a similar bill. Neither made it out of committee.

In April 2009 Senator Russell Feingold, a Wisconsin Democrat, introduced a new version of the Clean Water Restoration bill. The bill included a provision that removed the Court-ordered exemptions on nonnavigable waters and extended federal regulation to wetlands, small ponds, and streams. Farmers, small businesses, land-rights proponents, contractors, manufacturers, and representatives of other industries opposed the bill on grounds that it gave the federal government excessive regulatory authority. Such disproportionate power, they said, could put firms out of business, cost jobs, place undue financial burdens on farmers, and violate property owners' rights.

Proponents of the revisions said the new law was vital to protect the purity of the nation's water. "Every day Congress fails to reaffirm Clean Water Act protections, more and more waters are stripped of their protections, jeopardizing the drinking water of millions of Americans, as well as our nation's wildlife habitats, recreational pursuits, agricultural and industrial uses, and public health," Senator Feingold told his colleagues when introducing the bill.

MASSIVE OIL SPILL

As 2011 drew near, the goals of the Clean Water Act—to cleanse America's waters and make all its rivers and streams safe for swimming and fishing—had not yet been achieved. Many waterways remained polluted. Fish still were contaminated by mercury. Wastewater-treatment plants financed under the act were in need of repair and improvement. Many, unable to handle overflows from rainy weather, allowed raw sewage to escape into rivers and streams, where bacterial contaminants produced rashes and illness in swimmers.

On April 20, 2010, an offshore oil rig leased to British Petroleum (BP), one of the world's biggest energy companies, exploded off the Louisiana coast. The oil spill that resulted has been characterized by a number of politicians as the worst accidental marine spill in history. For the next hundred days, oil from the deep well sunk by the damaged rig, the *Deepwater Horizon*, flowed into the Gulf of Mexico. By the time the well was capped and the gushing stopped, almost five million barrels of oil had poured into the gulf's waters.

Eleven workers lost their lives in the initial explosion. Other victims included wildlife killed by the oil and animals whose habitats were destroyed. The spill and the massive cleanup costs associated with it have had a significant impact on everyone affected by it: the fishing and shrimping industries, municipalities faced with monumental cleanup costs, and businesses in the region, most notably firms dependent on tourism. All suffered economic losses. Scientists have yet to determine the long-term effects of oil that remains deep underwater in the Gulf.

Fire boats battle the blaze erupting from BP's offshore oil rig on April 21, 2010, in the Gulf of Mexico.

Under provisions of the Clean Water Act, BP might face as much as $21 billion in fines. Damage to wildlife and violations of other laws could result in additional penalties and fines. In June BP complied with an Obama administration demand that the oil company set up a $20 billion fund to reimburse those whose lives or businesses were disrupted by the spill. The government continued its investigation into the causes of the spill as the nation coped with the damage that resulted.

The BP spill put the spotlight on the importance of clean water. On April 21, 2010, the day after the disaster, Representative Oberstar introduced another clean-water bill in the House. Titled "America's Commitment to Clean Water Act," the bill encompassed many of the provisions in previous bills. Oberstar claimed that the bill did not expand federal power over waterways. "Restoring the Clean Water Act is only an expansion to the extent the Supreme Court ignored the intent of Congress and 30 years of precedent by narrowing the Act," Oberstar said. "Simply put, if it was not regulated before 2001, it will not be regulated with the enactment of this legislation."

Congress has introduced a number of bills to amend the Clean Air Act as well. The Clean Air Act amendments of 2010 required coal-fired power plants to cut mercury emissions by 90 percent and placed limits on emissions of sulfur dioxide and nitrogen oxides, which react to form ozone. "It is imperative to cut deadly emissions from our nation's fossil-fuel power plants," said Senator Thomas Carper, a Delaware Democrat, who introduced the bill. "We can't afford to wait any longer."

None of the clean-air and clean-water amendments had passed Congress when this book went to press. A change in the political makeup in the 112th Congress cast doubt on whether lawmakers would support any iniatives on clean air, clean water, or clean energy during the session. In the 2010 midterm elections, Republicans took control of the House and defeated a number of proenvironmental Democrats, including Feingold and Oberstar, sponsors of the Clean Water Restoration Act. Democrats lost six seats in the Senate, but retained a majority there.

GOOD NEWS

The pollution problem and its effects on the earth become more complex with each passing year. Even with setbacks and uncertainties, however, the Clean Air and Clean Water acts have contributed, in the years since their enactment, to efforts to improve the environment and protect Americans' health. In the view of many, if these acts had not been passed, America might have had undrinkable water and unbreathable air in large parts of the country. Problems that now look difficult to resolve might have been overwhelming, if not insurmountable.

The EPA says that America's air quality has "improved significantly" since 1970. By 2005, more than 75 percent of the country had met national air-quality standards. The results of the EPA's subsequent monitoring tests showed reductions in six major air pollutants. Between 1990 and 2007 ozone declined by 9 percent, particulates by 11 percent, lead by 80 percent, nitrogen dioxide by 35 percent, carbon monoxide by 67 percent, and sulfur dioxide (a key component of acid rain) by 54 percent. Since 1980 total emissions of these pollutants declined by more than 50 percent, the EPA reported.

Several studies have shown that the Clean Air Act's efforts to reduce air pollution have paid off in improved health of Americans. In 2009 the results of a study published in the *New England Journal of Medicine* showed that Americans are living five months longer because of improvements in air quality. "We did an intervention—improved air quality—and the question is, 'Did we get a return?'" wrote C. Arden Pope, who led the study. "The bottom line is yes, it looks like we did. Our efforts to clean up the air are helping."

Marking the Clean Air Act's fortieth birthday in September 2010, EPA administrator Lisa Jackson called the legislation "literally a life-saver." She estimated that the law has pre-vented tens of thousands of premature deaths every year and has improved the health of people with asthma, heart disease, and numerous other health conditions.

Jackson also asserted that the Clean Air Act is "one of the most cost-effective" pieces of legislation. The act's role in reducing air pollution, she said, has netted trillions of dol-lars in health benefits for Americans, keeping students in school and workers on the job and reducing the need for costly hospital stays and medications. "For every one dollar we as a nation have spent [on Clean Air Act regulations], we get more than $40 of benefits in return," she said.

Prodded by the Clean Air and Clean Water acts, industrial researchers developed several new antipollution devices and methods. Scientists at Carnegie Mellon University concluded that the 1970 Clean Air Act, in particular, "led to significant technological advances and environmental improvements." The results, the scientists acknowledged, also depended on the political and economic conditions of the time, which rein-forced EPA's pressure on industry to meet the regulations.

The Clean Water Act's advocates credit it with restoring to health the nation's rivers, lakes, streams, and ocean shores. Within a single generation, they say, America's waterways changed course. After a decline in quality that began in the mid–1800s and had seemed irreversible, the nation's waters again yield thriving fish stocks, fresh drinking water, and clean recreational spots.

The Clean Water Act forestalled the dumping of billions of pounds of wastes into waterways. In 2000, publicly owned plants were treating more than 40 billion gallons of waste-water a day. Sewage-treatment plants served only 85 million Americans in 1972; that number had doubled by 1996.

There have been many success stories. In the early 1970s, New York City's East River registered levels of bacteria from human and animal wastes at 160,000 organisms per 100 milliliters of water. In 2010 the bacteria levels tested at just 100 per 100 milliliters of water. The Merrimack River in New Hampshire is another river rescued by the Clean Water Act. Chuck Mower, who has lived along the banks of the river all his life, remembers when factories discharged industrial waste and cities dumped raw sewage into its waters. Back then, the sickly green river was thick and slimy, with waste coating everything on its surface. Mower now can paddle his canoe through the river's blue waters and see fish swimming along its bottom. Instead of gooey chunks of refuse, river grasses protrude from the water.

In 1972 only 36 percent of the nation's rivers and lakes were considered safe enough to fish and swim in. In 2010 people could swim and fish safely in more than 60 percent of America's waters. In its April 2009 edition, *New England Game & Fish* magazine cited the Androscoggin River—once among the nation's ten dirtiest rivers—as "perhaps the premier rainbow and brook trout river in Maine" and among the top trout rivers in the north country.

George J. Mitchell, who later became secretary of state, served as Muskie's administrative assistant from 1962 to 1965 and worked on the clean-air and clean-water bills. As a senator from Maine who filled Muskie's old seat, Mitchell later guided the 1987 amendments to the Clean Water Act and the 1990 amendments to the Clean Air Act through Congress. Mitchell noted that the nation's waters were much cleaner today as a result of the legislation. "Any American who wants to know what Ed Muskie's legacy is need only go to the nearest river," he said in remarks honoring Muskie

Boaters enjoy paddling along the Merrimack River in Canterbury, New Hampshire, in 2010.

after his death in 1996. "Before Ed Muskie, it was almost surely not fit to drink or to swim or to fish in. Because of Ed Muskie, it is now almost surely clean."

Senator Muskie believed that the goals of the Clean Water and Clean Air acts would stand the test of time and that the gains the legislation would yield were well worth the effort, the time, and the cost required. "A great nation cannot be measured solely in terms of its industrial capacity and Gross National Product," he concluded. "Ultimately our progress as a nation will be measured by how well we preserve and improve our own quality of life and that of future generations."

From Bill to Law

For a proposal to become a federal law, it must go through many steps:

In Congress:

1. A bill is proposed by a citizen, a legislator, the president, or another interested party. Most bills originate in the House and then are considered in the Senate.

2. A representative submits the bill to the House (the first reading). A senator submits it to the Senate. The person (or people) who introduces the bill is its main sponsor. Other lawmakers can become sponsors to show support for the bill. Each bill is read three times before the House or the Senate.

3. The bill is assigned a number and referred to the committee(s) and subcommittee(s) dealing with the topic. Each committee adopts its own rules, following guidelines of the House and the Senate. The committee chair controls scheduling for the bill.

4. The committees hold hearings if the bill is controversial or complex. Experts and members of the public may testify. Congress may compel witnesses to testify if they do not do so voluntarily.

5. The committee reviews the bill, discusses it, adds amendments, and makes other changes it deems necessary during markup sessions.

6. The committee votes on whether to support the bill, oppose it, or take no action on it and issues a report on its findings and recommendations.

7. A bill that receives a favorable committee report goes to the Rules Committee to be scheduled for consideration by the full House or Senate.

8. If the committee delays a bill or if the **Rules Committee** fails to schedule it, House members can sign a discharge motion and call for a vote on the matter. If a majority votes to release the bill from committee, it is scheduled on the calendar as any other bill would be. Senators may vote to discharge the bill from a committee as well. More commonly, though, a senator will add the bill as an amendment to an unrelated bill in order to get it past the committee blocking it. Or a senator can request that a bill be put directly on the Senate calendar, where it will be scheduled for debate. House and Senate members can also vote to suspend the rules and vote directly on a bill. Bills passed in this way must receive support from two thirds of those voting.

9. Members of both houses debate the bill. In the House, a chairperson moderates the discussion and each speaker's time is limited. Senators can speak on the issue for as long as they wish. Senators who want to block the bill may debate for hours in a tactic known as a filibuster. A three-fifths vote of the Senate is required to stop the filibuster (cloture), and talk on the bill is then limited to one hour per senator.

10. Following the debate, the bill is read section by section (the second reading). Members may propose amendments, which are voted on before the final bill comes up for a vote.

11. The full House and Senate then debate the entire bill and those amendments approved previously. Debate continues until a majority of members vote to "move the previous question" or approve a special resolution forcing a vote.

12. A full quorum—at least 218 members in the House, 51 in the Senate—must be present for a vote to be held. A member may request a formal count of members to ensure a quorum is on hand. Absent members are sought when there is no quorum.

13. Before final passage, opponents are given a last chance to propose amendments that alter the bill; the members vote on them.

14. A bill needs approval from a majority of those voting to pass. Members who do not want to take a stand on the issue may choose to abstain (not vote at all) or merely vote present.

15. If the House passes the bill, it goes on to the Senate. By that time, bills often have more than one hundred amendments attached to them. Occasionally, a Senate bill will go to the House.

16. If the bill passes in the same form in both the House and the Senate, it is sent to the clerk to be recorded.

17. If the Senate and the House version differ, the Senate sends the bill to the House with the request that members approve the changes.

18. If the two houses disagree on the changes, the bill may go to conference, where members appointed by the House and the Senate work out a compromise if possible.

19. The House and the Senate vote on the revised bill agreed to in conference. Further amendments may be added and the process repeated if the Senate and the House version of the bill differ.

20. The bill goes to the president for a signature.

To the President:

1. If the president signs the bill, it becomes law.

2. If the president vetoes the bill, it goes back to Congress, which can override his veto with a two-thirds vote in both houses.

3. If the president takes no action, the bill automatically becomes law after ten days if Congress is still in session.

4. If Congress adjourns and the president has taken no action on the bill within ten days, it does not become law. This is known as a pocket veto.

The time from introduction of the bill to the signing can range from several months to the entire two-year session. If a bill does not win approval during the session, it can be reintroduced in the next Congress, where it will have to go through the whole process again.

Glossary

acid rain—Rain that is made up of nitric and sulfuric acids; causes damage to plants, crops, and forests; poisons fish; contaminates water sources for animals and birds; and has been implicated in heart and lung diseases in humans.

air pollution—Contamination of air from harmful chemicals, gases, and other substances.

cap and trade—A system that limits total emissions allowed an industry, with each company allotted a percentage of the emissions. Companies with low emissions can sell their allotment to firms that require more than their share.

carbon dioxide—A colorless, odorless gas found naturally and released into the atmosphere by burning fossil fuels.

carbon monoxide—A colorless, odorless gas caused when hydrocarbon fuels do not completely burn. Carbon monoxide affects human health and can lead to death in some cases. Most carbon monoxide emissions come from motor vehicles.

catalytic converter—A device built into motor vehicles that reduces harmful emissions.

DDT (dichlorodiphenyltrichloroethane)—A toxic pesticide banned in 1972 after it was linked to cancer and other diseases in humans.

discharges—Chemicals, wastes, and other substances dumped into the water.

emissions—Gases, particles, and other substances released into the air by automobiles, smokestacks, and the like.

global warming—A rise in temperature of the earth's surface, caused in modern times mostly by the release of greenhouse gases into the atmosphere (see greenhouse gases).

greenhouse gases—Gases in the air such as carbon dioxide, methane, chlorofluorocarbons, nitrous oxide, ozone, and water vapor that trap the sun's heat and cause a rise in the earth's temperature (see global warming).

groundwater—Water that flows underground and supplies a good portion of the world's drinking water.

hydrocarbons—Compounds made up of hydrogen and carbon atoms; the major components of smog and greenhouse gases (see greenhouse gases, smog).

nitrogen oxides—Compounds that contribute to smog and acid rain; linked to cancer, heart disease, and other health problems in humans.

ozone—A strong smelling, pale blue toxic gas that is the main component of smog.

particulate matter—Any material, except pure water, that exists in the solid or liquid state in the atmosphere. The size of particulate matter can vary from coarse, wind-blown dust particles to fine particle combustion products.

pollution—Waste material, chemicals, or other substances that worsen the quality of air, water, or earth.

runoff—Water from rain or snow that flows from the land into lakes, rivers, and streams.

sewage treatment plant—A system that removes toxins from human waste and other waste material.

smog—A low-lying cloud formed primarily from automobile emissions and composed of carbon monoxide, hydrocarbons, sulfur oxides, nitrogen oxides, water drops, and solid particles suspended in air. The word "smog" is a combination of "fog" and "smoke," first used in 1905 by a London scientist.

toxic hot spot—A concentration of heavy metals, chemicals, or other toxins in the water or the air.

wastewater—Dirty water discharged from homes, businesses, and industries, for example, sewage and industrial wastes.

water pollution—Contamination of water from harmful chemicals, untreated sewage, industrial wastes, and other substances.

wetlands—Areas such as swamps, marshes, bogs, and similar locales that are usually wet and that support aquatic plants and animals.

ABBREVIATED TERMS

CWA—Clean Water Act

CAA—Clean Air Act

CEQ—Council on Environmental Quality, formed to advise the president on environmental affairs

EPA—U.S. Environmental Protection Agency, department in charge of environmental issues and regulation

HEW—U.S. Department of Health, Education, and Welfare. In 1980 it was divided into two departments, the Department of Health and Human Services and the Department of Education.

NEPA—National Environmental Policy Act

Notes

Introduction

p. 7, "no thicker than . . .": Leon Billings, "Edmund S. Muskie: Late a Senator from Maine: Memorial Tributes," S. Doc. 104–17, Washington, DC: U.S. GPO, 1996, http://bulk.resource.org/gpo.gov/documents/104/sd017.pdf

Chapter One

p. 14, "No two factors . . .": George M. Koker, "Oration: The Progress and Tendency of Hygiene and Sanitary Science in the Nineteenth Century," *Journal of the American Medical Association* (June 8, 1901): 1617–1626.

p. 15, "One of the most pressing . . .": Koker, "Oration."

p. 16, "In a unanimous . . .": *Missouri v. Illinois*, 200 US 496 (1906).

p. 16, "The *New York Times* reported . . .": "Death in the Streets," *New York Times*, March 13, 1871, 10.

p. 17, "It is rare . . .": "Sanitary Supervision," *New York Times*, May 24, 1878, 4.

p. 18, "Dead cats . . .": "Letters to the Editor: Impure Croton," *New York Times*, April 20, 1979, 10.

p. 20, "increased the fire . . .": "Plea for Clean Beaches," *New York Times*, October 26, 1921, 28.

p. 21, "Government regulation alone . . .": Betsy McCully, "History of New York Habitats," New York Nature, www.newyorknature.net

p. 25, "national peril . . .": Paul P. Kennedy, "Resources Report Says Water Waste Is National Peril," *New York Times*, December 18, 1950, 1.

p. 25, "Grave as it is . . .": Kennedy, "Resources Report Says Water Waste Is National Peril."

p. 26, "treated the [antipollution] . . .": United Press International, "Anti-Pollution Plan Assailed," *New York Times*, December 20, 1955, 33.

p. 26, "a veto power . . .": Bess Furman, "Pollution Action Called Assured," *New York Times*, May 27, 1956, 35.

p. 27, "written consent . . .": John B. Oakes, "Conservation: Pollution Control," *New York Times*, June 3, 1956, 159.

p. 27, "still extremely tender . . .": Oakes, "Conservation: Pollution Control."

Chapter Two

p. 30, "During one of his . . .": Edmund S. Muskie, *Journeys*, New York: Doubleday, 1972, 8–9.

p. 32, "a cross between . . .": Katharine Whittemore, "Farewell to a Tailor's Son," Outtakes, Stephen O. Muskie, 1997 (originally published in *Yankee Magazine*). www.outtakes.com/tailor/farewell4.html

p. 32, "He could sit . . .": Leon Billings, author interview, February 17, 2009.

p. 32, "We put up with . . .": Mike Richard, interview with Charles Abbott, Edmund S. Muskie Archives and Special Collections Library, Bates College, http://digilib. bates.edu/cgi-bin/library.cgi

p. 33, "When I worked . . .": Muskie, *Journeys*, 73.

p. 33, "That's when I began . . .": Chris Beam, interview with Edmund S. Muskie, Shep Lee, Don Nicoll, and Frank Coffin, Edmund S. Muskie Archives and Special Collections Library.

p. 35, "began in my backyard . . .": Muskie, *Journeys*, 95.

p. 37, "The water pollution program . . .": "Water Pollution Center of Fight," *New York Times*, (April 7, 1963, 73.

Chapter Three

p. 41, "The atmosphere over . . .": W. H. Lawrence, "President Offers Wide Health Plan with Reinsurance," *New York Times*, February 1, 1955, 1.

p. 42, "Can anyone believe . . .": Rachel Carson, *Silent Spring*, 40th anniv. ed., (New York: Mariner Books, 2002), 7–8.

p. 44, "the lore of . . .": "Rachel Carson Dies of Cancer," *New York Times*, April 15, 1964, cited in *The Life and Legacy of Rachel Carson*, www.RachelCarson.org

p. 45, "Chlorinated hydrocarbons . . .": Rachel Carson, "Miss Carson Objects," *New York Times*, June 18, 1963, 36.

p. 45, "Man is a part . . .": "Rachel Carson Dies of Cancer."

p. 46, "the right . . . to be secure . . .": Robert C. Toth, "Pesticide Peril Charged to U.S.," *New York Times*, June 5, 1963, 41.

p. 46, "We owe much . . .": Lyndon B. Johnson, "Remarks upon Signing the Pesticide Control Bill," American Presidency Project, May 12, 1964, www.presidency.ucsb. edu/ws/index.php?pid=26245

p. 47, "The notion . . .": Muskie, *Journeys*, 83.

p. 47, "Now is the time . . .": "New U.S. Bill Asks Pollution Penalties," *New York Times*, January 26, 1963, 1.

p. 47, "far outstretches . . .": Bernard Stengren, "It Was a Clear and Windy Day for a Look at the Smoke Problem Here," *New York Times*, September 14, 1963, 27.

p. 48, "We wanted . . .": Muskie, *Journeys*, 85.

p. 48, "Considering the present . . .": Evert Clark, "Celebrezze Asks Car-Fume Curbs, *New York Times*, January 5, 1965, 19.

p. 50, "20 or 30 years . . .": Cabell Phillips, "Administration Eases Its Stand on the Control of Air Pollution," *New York Times*, April 9, 1965, 38.

Chapter Four

p. 53, "It involves . . .": Lady Bird Johnson, "In Her Own Words," Lady Bird Johnson Final Tribute, Lady Bird Johnson Wildflower Center, www.ladybirdjohnsontribute. org/tribute_herwords.htm

p. 54, "The environment is where . . .": Lady Bird Johnson, "In Her Own Words."

p. 55, "No one has . . ."; Gladwin Hill, "New U.S. Agency and New Policy to Enter Fight Against Water Pollution," *New York Times*, December 21, 1965, 27.

p. 55–56, "barely sufficient . . .": Editorial, "Cleaning Up the Waters," *New York Times*, February 4, 1965, 30.

p. 56, "Our theory . . .": Gladwin Hill, "Pollution Curbs Fought in North," *New York Times*, March 15, 1965, 31.

p. 57, "the environmentalist . . .": Muskie, *Journeys*, 95.

p. 57, "Unless American . . .": Gladwin Hill, "New U.S. Agency and New Policy to Enter Fight Against Water Pollution."

p. 59, "the poor little . . .": Fred P. Graham, "Oil Pollution Act Is Found Crippled," *New York Times*, April 16, 1967, 41.

p. 59, "as much particulate . . .": Evert Clark, "Scientists Fear Nature May Win," *New York Times*, March 15, 1966, 19.

p. 60, "chocolate-brown . . .": "The Cities: The Price of Optimism," *Time*, August 1, 1969, www.time.com/time/magazine/article/0,9171,901182,00.html

p. 60, "Cleveland, even now . . .": Randy Newman, "Burn On," *Sail Away*, Rhino/WEA, www.randynewman.com/tocdiscography/disc_sail_away/lyricssailaway/?searchterm=Burn%20On,%20Big%20River%20lyrics

p. 60, "It's been an absolutely . . ."; Michael Scott, "After the Flames: The Story Behind the 1969 Cuyahoga River Fire and Its Recovery," *Plain Dealer*, January 4, 2009, blog.cleveland.com/metro/2009/01/after_the_flames_the_story_beh.html

p. 62, "legally declared . . .": "An Aroused Nation Seeks Billions to Dam the Rising Tide of Pollution," *New York Times*, January 6, 1969, 74.

p. 62, "put the environment . . .": "Gaylord Nelson," Wilderness Society, http://wilderness.org/content/gaylord-nelson

p. 62, "a turning point . . .": "A Memento Mori to the Earth," *Time*, May 4, 1970. www.time.com/time/magazine/article/0,9171,943782,00.html

p. 63, "one of the most remarkable . . .": "Gaylord Nelson," Wilderness Society.

p. 63, "increasingly incapable . . .": "A Memento Mori to the Earth."

p. 64, "Demonstrators conducted . . .": "A Memento Mori to the Earth."

p. 64, "You're next, people!": "A Memento Mori to the Earth."

p. 64, "the right to clean air . . .": Constitution of the Commonwealth of Massachusetts, www.mass.gov/legis/const.htm#cart097.htm

p. 66, "absolutely must be the years . . .": "Text of Nixon Statement," *New York Times*, January 2, 1970, 12.

p. 66, "The American people . . .": James Reston, "Washington: The Politics of Pollution," *New York Times*, April 26, 1970, E12.

Chapter Five

p. 69, "Air is our . . ."; "Text of the President's Message to Congress Proposing Action Against Pollution," *New York Times*, February 11, 1970, 32.

p. 70, "We know what...": Dennis Hevesi, "Paul G. Rogers, 'Mr. Health' in Congress, Is Dead at 87," *New York Times*, October 15, 2008, A29.

p. 70, "That kind of . . .": Albert Bozzo, "Breathing Easier Thanks to the Clear Air Act," CNBC.com

p. 70, "Many State health . . .": "Air pollution—1970. Hearings, Ninety-first Congress, second session," on S. 3229, S. 3466 [and] S. 3546, part 2, www.archive.org/stream/airpollution197002unit/airpollution197002unit_djvu.txt

p. 71, "If you want . . .": Rogers, Rogers, Paul G. "The Clean Air Act of 1970." *EPA Journal*, January/February 1990.

p. 74, "The bill took . . .": Billings interview with author.

p. 74, "Everyone understood . . .": cited in "Implementing Technology-Forcing Policies: The 1970 Clean Air Act Amendments and the Introduction of Advanced Automotive Emissions Controls," David Gerard and Lester B. Lave, Carnegie Mellon University, May 2003, www.epp.cmu.edu/httpdocs/people/bios/papers/gerard/Gerard_Lave%20TF1.pdf

p. 75, "They [the auto executives] . . .": Leon Billings interview by Don Nicoll. Muskie Oral History Project, Lewiston, ME: Muskie Archives and Special Collections Library, Bates College, September 16, 2002.

p. 75, "As far as . . .": E. W. Kenworthy, "Tough New Clean-Air Bill Passed by Senate, 73 to 0," New York Times, September 23, 1970, 1.

p. 76, "Ed, you finally . . .": Edmund S. Muskie, "NEPA to CERCLA: The Clean Air Act: A Commitment to Public Health," Environmental Forum, January/February 1990.

p. 77, "His favorite...": "Howard Baker," American Lawyer Hall of Fame, 2008, www.law.com/jsp/law/talhof/lawArticleHOF.jsp?id=1202424565252&r=lifetime/winners

p. 78, "I don't think . . .": Leon Billings interview by Don Nicoll, September 16, 2002.

p. 78, "year of the beginning . . .": James M. Naughton, "President Signs Bill to Cut Auto Fumes 90% by 1977," New York Times, January 1, 1971, 1.

p. 78, "watershed that paved . . .": Muskie, "NEPA to CERCLA: The Clean Air Act: A Commitment to Public Health."

p. 79, "In many respects . . .": Howard H. Baker Jr., "Cleaning America's Air—Progress and Challenges," speech, University of Tennessee, March 9, 2005, www.muskiefoundation.org/baker.030905.html

p. 79, "Air pollution provided . . .": Muskie, Journeys, 84.

p. 79–80, "began a process . . .": Muskie, "NEPA to CERCLA: The Clean Air Act: A Commitment to Public Health."

Chapter Six

p. 82, "It's an outrage . . .": E. W. Kenworthy. "Rep. Cramer Stiffens Stand on Oil Spillage," New York Times, February 18, 1970, 85.

p. 84, "What we think . . .": Muskie, Journeys, 89.

p. 86, "sufficiently awakened . . .": Bernard Asbell, The Senate Nobody Knows (Baltimore: Johns Hopkins University Press, 1978), 137.

p. 87, "well within . . .": E. W. Kenworthy, "Pollution Panel Foresees Gains," New York Times, August 7, 1971, 1.

p. 88, "The EPA can act . . .": William M. Blair, "Clean-Water Act Held Insufficient," New York Times, May 26, 1971, 84.

p. 89, "A massive . . .": E. W. Kenworthy, "House Approves Water Pollution Bill," New York Times, March 30, 1972, 18.

p. 92, "cancer of water pollution . . .": Congressional Record, "Proceedings and Debates of the 92nd Congress," Bill S. 2770, October 4, 1972, http://bulk.resource.org/courts.gov/juris/j1440_02.sgml

p. 93, "pay great and lasting dividends . . .": *Congressional Record*, "Proceedings and Debates of the 92nd Congress."

p. 93, "margin so overwhelming . . .": *Congressional Record*, "Proceedings and Debates of the 92nd Congress."

p. 94, "It seems reasonable . . .": E. W. Kenworthy, "Clean-Water Bill Is Law Despite President's Veto," *New York Times*, October 19, 1972, 26.

p. 94, "He said in a statement . . .": E. W. Kenworthy, "President Vetoes Clean Water Bill," *New York Times*, October 18, 1972, 20.

p. 94, "Can we afford . . .": *Congressional Record*, "Proceedings and Debates of the 92nd Congress."

p. 95, "Stinky Sludge . . .": Craig Rancourt, interview with author, February 9, 2009.

p. 95, "stinky, slow-moving . . .": Dan Tarkinson, "The Presumpscot: A New River," *Fly Fishing in Maine*, February 9, 2009, www.flyfishinginmaine.com/story. php?id=10

p. 96, "I feel we are . . .": *Congressional Record*, "Proceedings and Debates of the 92nd Congress."

p. 96, "far and away . . .": *Congressional Record*, "Proceedings and Debates of the 92nd Congress."

p. 96, "The Clean Water Act . . .": James L. Oberstar, "Statement of the Chairman, Committee on Transportation and Infrastructure," hearing on the Clean Water Restoration Act, April 16, 2008, http://transportation.house.gov/Media/File/ Full%20Committee/20080416/jlo%20open.pdf

Chapter Seven

p. 98, "Muskie, later admitting . . .": Muskie, "NEPA to CERCLA: The Clean Air Act: A Commitment to Public Health."

p. 99, "Certainly, knowledge . . .": Asbell, *The Senate Nobody Knows*, 88.

p. 102, "Ten years ago . . .": Tom Ferrell, "After 10 Years, Earth Day Again: How Well Are We Doing?" *New York Times*, April 22, 1980, E18.

p. 102, "Every new proposal . . .": Muskie, "Theodore Roosevelt once said, 'Americanism is a question of principle,'" *Boston Globe*, April 22, 1980, 1.

p. 102, "It will not . . .": Muskie, "Theodore Roosevelt once said, 'Americanism is a question of principle.'"

p. 104, "The concept . . .": Joanne Ditmer, "Raising the Roof Optimistic: Environmental activist perceives progress," *Denver Post*, April 26, 1992, 3.

p. 105, "part of the cost . . .": Keith Schneider, "Ideas & Trends: How Clean Air Became Part of the Bottom Line," *New York Times*, October 28, 1990, D4.

p. 105, "Some of our major progress . . .": Ditmer, "Raising the Roof Optimistic: Environmental activist perceives progress."

p. 106, "The U.S. EPA . . .": Erin Kelly, "U.S. Waterways Remain Polluted," Gannett News Service, July 25, 2000.

p. 110, "This is the single . . .": John M. Broder, "Obama to Toughen Rules on Emissions and Mileage," *New York Times*, May 19, 2009, 1.

p. 110, "a huge step forward": "The Earth Wins One," *New York Times*, May 20, 2009, A28.

p. 110, "to keep pushing . . .": Julie Pace, "Obama still supports climate legislation," Associated Press, July 27, 2010.

p. 111, "We are in essence . . . ": Charles Duhigg and Janet Roberts, "Rulings Restrict Clean Water Act, Foiling E.P.A.," *New York Times*, March 1, 2010, A1.

p. 111, "We need something . . . ": Duhigg and Roberts, "Rulings Restrict Clean Water Act, Foiling E.P.A."

p. 111–112, "did not intend . . . ": Duhigg and Roberts, "Rulings Restrict Clean Water Act, Foiling E.P.A."

p. 112, "Every day Congress . . .": "Feingold Reintroduces Effort to Protect the Drinking Water of over 100 Million Americans," Senate press release (April 2, 2009).

p. 115, "Restoring the Clean Water . . .": James L. Oberstar, "Introduction of H.R. 5088, America's Commitment to Clean Water Act," *Congressional Record*, 111th Cong., 2nd sess., April 21, 2010, E608–E609.

p. 115, "It is imperative . . .": Thomas Carper, "American Lung Association Report Warns That More Than Half of All Americans Exposed to Air Too Dangerous to Breathe." Press release, April 28, 2010, http://carper.senate.gov/press/record.cfm?id=324310

p. 116, "We did an intervention . . .": Nicholas Bakalar, "Cleaner Air Found to Add 5 Months to Life," *New York Times*, January 21, 2009, D6.

p. 117, "led to significant . . .": Gerard and Lave, "Implementing Technology-Forcing Policies: The 1970 Clean Air Act Amendments and the Introduction of Advanced Automotive Emissions Control."

p. 117, "one of the most cost-effective . . .": Lisa P. Jackson address: "The 40th Anniversary of the Clean Air Act," US EPA video, September 14, 2010. http://www.ustream.tv/recorded/9567909

p. 117, "For every one dollar . . .": Lisa P. Jackson address.

p. 118, "perhaps the premier . . .": Al Raychard, "Our Top North Country Trout Rivers," *New England Game & Fish*, April 2009, www.newenglandgameandfish.com/fishing/trout-fishing/NG_0409_02/#close

p. 118–119, "Any American . . .": Andy Thibault, "Muskie Eulogized as Environmentalist, Negotiator," *Washington Times*, March 31, 1996, A3.

p. 119, "A great nation . . .": Muskie, "NEPA to CERCLA: The Clean Air Act: A Commitment to Public Health."

All websites were available and accurate as of November 8, 2010.

Further Information

Audio/Video

ABC News Classroom: Global Warming: Rising Temperatures, Rising Fears. DVD. Disney Educational Productions, 2006.

Eyes of Nye: Transportation. DVD. Disney Educational Productions, 2005.

An Inconvenient Truth. DVD. Paramount. 2006.

The Legislative Branch (U.S. Government). DVD. Schlessinger Media, 2002.

Schoolhouse Rock: Earth. DVD. Disney Educational Productions. 2009.

Books

Calhoun, Yael, ed. *Water Pollution.* Environmental Issues. Broomall, PA: Chelsea House, 2004.

Carson, Rachel. *Silent Spring.* New York: Mariner Books, 2002. Reprint.

Chehoski, Robert, ed. *Critical Perspectives on Climate Disruption.* Critical Anthologies of Nonfiction Writing. New York: Rosen Central, 2006.

Gerdes, Louise I., ed. *Pollution.* Opposing Viewpoints. Farmington Hills, MI: Greenhaven Press, 2005.

Hamilton, Lee H. *How Congress Works and Why You Should Care.* Bloomington: Indiana University Press, 2004.

Kidd, J. S., and Renee A. Kidd. *Air Pollution: Problems and Solutions.* Science and Society. New York: Facts on File, 2005.

Nakaya, Andrea C., ed. *Is Air Pollution a Serious Threat to Health?* Farmington Hills, MI: Greenhaven Press, 2004.

Rapp, Valerie. *Protecting Earth's Air Quality.* Saving Our Living Earth. Minneapolis: Lerner, 2008.

Steffof, Rebecca. *Preserving the Living Earth*. New York: Benchmark Books, 2011.

Tanaka, Shelley. *Climate Change*. Groundwork Guides. La Jolla, CA: Groundwork Books, 2007.

WEBSITES
American Meteorological Society: History of the Clean Air Act
www.ametsoc.org/Sloan/cleanair/index.html

Ben's Guide to U.S. Government for Kids
http://bensguide.gpo.gov/

Dirksen Congressional Center
www.congresslink.org

Edmund S. Muskie Archives and Special Collections
http://abacus.bates.edu/muskie-archives/

Edmund S. Muskie Foundation
www.muskiefoundation.org/

Govtrack.us: A Civic Project to Track Congress
www.govtrack.us/congress/legislation.xpd

Library of Congress, American Memory section
http://memory.loc.gov/ammem/collections

Muskie School of Public Service
http://muskie.usm.maine.edu

National Archives and Records Administration
www.archives.gov

U.S. Environmental Protection Agency
www.epa.gov

U.S. House of Representatives
www.house.gov/

U.S. Senate
www.senate.gov/

Bibliography

ARTICLES/SPEECHES

"An Aroused Nation Seeks Billions to Dam the Rising Tide of Pollution." *New York Times*, January 6, 1969.

Andreen, William L. "The Evolution of Water Pollution Control in the United States—State, Local, and Federal Efforts, 1789–1972: Part II." *Stanford Environmental Law Journal* 22 (July 22, 2003): 215–294.

———. "Water Quality Today—Has the Clean Water Act Been a Success?" *Alabama Law Review* 55 (2004): 537–593.

Associated Press. "Miss Carson Describes Rise in Chemical Poison." *New York Times*, June 7, 1963.

Bailey, Ronald. "Earth Day, Then and Now." *Reason*, May 2000.

Bakalar, Nicholas. "Cleaner Air Found to Add 5 Months to Life." *New York Times*, January 21, 2009.

Baker, Howard. "Cleaning America's Air—Progress and Challenges." Speech, University of Tennessee, Knoxville, March 9, 2005. http://www.muskie foundation.org/baker.030905.html

Blair, William M. "Clean-Water Act Held Insufficient." *New York Times*, May 26, 1971.

———. "House Approves a Clean Air Bill." *New York Times*, November 3, 1967.

Bozzo, Albert. "Breathing Easier Thanks to the Clear Air Act." CNBC.com, November 2, 2007.

Broder, John M. "Obama's Order Likely to Tighten Auto Standards." *New York Times*, January 27, 2009.

———. "Obama to Toughen Rules on Emissions and Mileage." *New York Times*. May 19, 2009.

Carson, Rachel. "Miss Carson Objects." *New York Times*, June 18, 1963.

"The Cities: The Price of Optimism." *Time*, August 1, 1969. www.time.com/time/ magazine/article/0,9171,901182,00.html

Clark, Evert. "Celebrezze Asks Car-Fume Curbs." *New York Times*, January 5, 1965.

———. "Scientists Fear Nature May Win." *New York Times*, March 15, 1966.

"Cleaning Up the Waters." *New York Times*, February 4, 1965.

"A Clear, Clean Water Act." *New York Times*, April 17, 2009.

Cochran, Rod. "Maine's Androscoggin River Comeback." *New England Game and Fish*, May 25, 2009. www.newenglandgameandfish.com/fishing/trout-fishing/ng_aa063304a

"Critic of Pesticides; Rachel Louise Carson." Obituary. *New York Times*, April 15, 1964.

Dean, Clarence. "Clams on Market Called Safe Now." *New York Times*, August 24, 1961.

"Death in the Streets." *New York Times*, March 13, 1871.

"Demand Action on Oil Pollution Bill." *New York Times*, August 12, 1922.

Ditmer, Joanne. "Raising the Roof Optimistic: Environmental activist perceives progress." *Denver Post*. April 26, 1992.

Doty, Robert C. "Pollution Halved in 13 Years by Joint Efforts of Three States." *New York Times*, August 28, 1950.

Douglas, Kristen. "An Environmental Bill of Rights for Canada." Law and Government Division, November 1991.

"The Earth Wins One." *New York Times*, May 20, 2009.

"Edmund S. Muskie: Late a Senator from Maine: Memorial Tributes." S. Doc. 104–117, Washington, DC: U.S. GPO, 1996.

"EPA Celebrates 15th Anniversary of Clean Air Act Amendments." EPA news release, November 15, 2005.

"Feingold Reintroduces Effort to Protect the Drinking Water of over 100 Million Americans." Senate press release, April 2, 2009.

Ferrell, Tom. "After 10 Years, Earth Day Again: How Well Are We Doing?" *New York Times*, April 22, 1980.

Fleming, James R., and Bethany R. Knorr. "History of the Clean Air Act." American Meteorological Society. www.ametsoc.org/Sloan/cleanair/index.html

Furman, Bess. "Pollution Action Called Assured." *New York Times*, May 27, 1956.

"Gaylord Nelson." Wilderness Society. http://wilderness.org

Gerard, David, and Lester B. Lave. "Implementing Technology-Forcing Policies: The 1970 Clean Air Act Amendments and the Introduction of Advanced Automotive Emissions Controls." Center for the Study and Improvement of Regulation, Carnegie Mellon University, May 2003.

Graham, Fred P. "Oil Pollution Act Is Found Crippled." *New York Times*, April 16, 1967.

"Greenhouse Gases, Climate Change, and Energy." U.S. Department of Energy, May 2008.

Grutzner, Charles. "Economic Toll of City's Dirty Air Is Put at $520 Million Annually." *New York Times*, April 8, 1965.

Harding, Anne. "Drop in U.S. Air Pollution Linked to Longer Lifespans." CNNhealth.com, January 21, 2009. www.cnn.com/2009/HEALTH/01/21/healthmag.airpollution.lifespan

Hill, Gladwin. "New U.S. Agency and New Policy to Enter Fight against Water Pollution." *New York Times*, December 21, 1965.

———. "Pollution Curbs Fought in North." *New York Times*, March 15, 1965.

———. "Smog and Ire Fill Los Angeles Air." *New York Times*, October 17, 1954.

Hoffman, Jascha. "Criminal Element." *New York Times Magazine*, October 21, 2007.

"Howard Baker." American Lawyer Hall of Fame, 2008.

"Impure Croton." Letter to the editor. *New York Times*, April 20, 1979.

Johnson, Lady Bird. "In Her Own Words." Lady Bird Johnson Final Tribute, Lady Bird Johnson Wildflower Center. www.ladybirdjohnsontribute.org/tribute_herwords.htm

Johnson, Lyndon B. "Remarks upon Signing the Pesticide Control Bill." *American Presidency Project*, May 12, 1964. www.presidency.ucsb.edu/ws/index.php?pid=26245

Jones, David R. "Auto Men Testify on Smog Devices." *New York Times*, April 8, 1965.

Kelley, Tim. "Reading the River and Its Contents, with an Eye on Its Health." *New York Times*, July 24, 2008.

Kelly, Erin. "U.S. Waterways Remain Polluted." Gannett News Service, July 25, 2000.

Kennedy, Paul P. "Resources Report Says Water Waste Is National Peril." *New York Times*, December 18, 1950.

Kenworthy, E. W. "Clean-Water Bill Is Law despite President's Veto." *New York Times*, October 19, 1972.

———. "House Approves Water Pollution Bill." *New York Times*, March 30, 1972.

———. "Muskie Introduces $25-Billion Water Pollution Control Measure." *New York Times*, February 3, 1971.

———. "Panel to Study Change in Pollution Bill." *New York Times*, March 1, 1971.

———. "Pollution Panel Foresees Gains." *New York Times*, August 7, 1971.

———. "President Vetoes Clean Water Bill." *New York Times*, October 18, 1972.

———. "Rep. Cramer Stiffens Stand on Oil Spillage." *New York Times*, February 18, 1970.

———. "Tough New Clean-Air Bill Passed by Senate, 73 to 0." *New York Times*, September 23, 1970.

Koker, George M. "Oration: The Progress and Tendency of Hygiene and Sanitary Science in the Nineteenth Century." *Journal of the American Medical Association* (June 8, 1901): 1617–1626.

Kovarik, Bill. "Oil Pollution and the National Coast Anti-Pollution League." *Environmental History Timeline*. www.runet.edu/~wkovarik/envhist/coast.html

Krebs, Albin, and Robert M. Thomas Jr. "Notes on People; Muskie Recovering." *New York Times*, February 10, 1982.

Laurence, William L. "Parran Urges End of River Pollution." *New York Times*, April 18, 1947.

Lawrence, W. H. "President Offers Wide Health Plan with Reinsurance." *New York Times*, February 1, 1955.

Lelyveld, Joseph. "Millions Join Earth Day Observances across the Nation." *New York Times*, April 23, 1970.

"Letters to the Editor: Impure Croton," *New York Times*, April 20, 1979, 10.

McCully, Betsy. "History of New York Habitats." New York Nature. www.newyorknature.net.

McMurtry, Virginia. "Impoundments." *CRS Report* RL33635, January 12, 2009.

"A Memento Mori to the Earth." *Time*, May 4, 1970.

Michaels, Patricia A. "Air Pollution: Legislative History before the Clean Air Act." *Green Nature*, 2000. http://greennature.com/article246.html

Muskie, Edmund S. "NEPA to CERCLA: The Clean Air Act: A Commitment to Public Health." *Environmental Forum*, January/February 1990.

"National Air Quality—Status and Trends through 2007." U.S. Environmental Protection Agency, 2008.

Naughton, James M. "President Signs Bill to Cut Auto Fumes 90% by 1977." *New York Times*, January 1, 1971.

"New Report Shows Benefits of 1990 Clean Air Act Amendments Outweigh Costs by Four-to-One Margin." Environmental Protection Agency press release, November 16, 1999.

"New U.S. Bill Asks Pollution Penalties." *New York Times*, January 26, 1963.

Oakes, John B. "Conservation: Pollution Control." *New York Times*, June 3, 1956.

Oberstar, James L. "Statement of the Chairman, Committee on Transportation and Infrastructure." Hearing on the Clean Water Restoration Act, April 16, 2008.

Phillips, Cabell. "Administration Eases Its Stand on the Control of Air Pollution." *New York Times*, April 9, 1965.

———. "Health Aide Cool to Antismog Bill." *New York Times*, April 7, 1965.

"Plea for Clean Beaches." *New York Times*, October 26, 1921.

"Pollution Bill Signed." *New York Times*, July 1, 1948.

"President Signs Bill to Control Automobile Exhaust Impurities." *New York Times*, October 21, 1965.

"Rachel Carson Dies of Cancer." *New York Times*, April 15, 1964.

Raychard, Al. "Our Top North Country Trout Rivers." *New England Fish and Game*, April 2009.

Reston, James. "Washington: The Politics of Pollution." *New York Times*, April 26, 1970.

Rogers, Paul G. "The Clean Air Act of 1970." *EPA Journal*, January/February 1990.

"Sanitary Supervision." *New York Times*, May 24, 1878.

Schneider, Keith. "Ideas & Trends: How Clean Air Became Part of the Bottom Line." *New York Times*, October 28, 1990.

Scott, Michael. "After the Flames: The Story behind the 1969 Cuyahoga River Fire and Its Recovery." *Cleveland Plain Dealer*, January 4, 2009.

Semple, Robert B., Jr. "President Orders Curbs on Dumping in U.S. Waterways." *New York Times*, December 24, 1970.

Shabecoff, Philip. "Congress Votes Clean Water Rules." *New York Times*, December 16, 1977.

Shapiro-Shapin, Carolyn G. "A Really Excellent Scientific Contribution: Scientific Creativity, Scientific Professionalism, and the Chicago Drainage Case, 1900–1906." *Bulletin of the History of Medicine* 71, no. 3 (1997): 385–411.

Smith, Hal H. "Summary of Important Legislation Passed in 3rd Session of 75th Congress." *New York Times*, June 17, 1938.

"Smoke—A Warning." *New York Times*, November 24, 1953.

Stengren, Bernard. "It Was a Clear and Windy Day for a Look at the Smoke Problem Here." *New York Times*, September 14, 1963.

Sullivan, Walter. "Man Must Re-Use Wastes, Pollution Report Asserts." *New York Times*, April 1, 1966.

"Supply of Water Found Dwindling." *New York Times*, January 17, 1947.

Tarkinson, Dan. "The Presumpscot: A New River." *Fly Fishing in Maine*, February 9, 2009.

"Text of Nixon Statement." *New York Times*, January 2, 1970.

"Text of the President's Message to Congress Proposing Action against Pollution." *New York Times*, February 11, 1970.

Thibault, Andy. "Muskie Eulogized as Environmentalist, Negotiator." *Washington Times*, March 31, 1996.

Toth, Robert C. "Pesticide Peril Charged to U.S." *New York Times*, June 5, 1963.

Trussell, C. P. "Senate Combats Water Pollution." *New York Times*, October 17, 1963.

United Press International. "Anti-Pollution Plan Assailed." *New York Times*, December 20, 1955.

———. "Pollution Laws Called a Threat to Industries." *New York Times*, May 19, 1971.

"U.S. Wastewater Treatment." Center for Sustainable Systems, University of Michigan. 2009.

Van Noppen, Trip. "Fixing the Broken Clean Water Act." *Unearthed*. Earthjustice Forum, February 17, 2009, http://unearthed.earthjustice.org/blog/2009-february/fixing-broken-clean-water-act?page=1

Wachs, Martin, and Jennifer Dill. "Regionalism in Transportation and Air Quality: History, Interpretation, and the Insights for Regional Governance." Committee on Metropolitan Governance, National Academy of Sciences. September 1997.

Walsh, Bryan. "George W. Bush's Last Environmental Stand." *Time*, November 5, 2008.

———. "Lisa Jackson: The New Head of the EPA." *Time*, April 23, 2009.

———. "Obama Cleans Up after Bush." *Time*, January 24, 2009.

"Water Pollution Center of Fight." *New York Times*, April 7, 1963.

Whittemore, Katharine. "Farewell to a Tailor's Son." *Outtakes* (Stephen O. Muskie's website). 1997. www.outtakes.com/tailor/farewell4.html Originally published in *Yankee* magazine.

BOOKS

Asbell, Bernard. *The Senate Nobody Knows*. New York: Doubleday, 1978.

Carson, Rachel. *Silent Spring*. 40th anniv. ed. New York: Mariner Books, 2002.

Doyle, Jack. *Taken for a Ride: Detroit's Big Three and the Politics of Pollution*. New York: Four Walls Eight Windows, 2000.

Lear, Linda. *Rachel Carson: Witness for Nature*. New York: Mariner Books, 2009.

Milazzo, Paul. *Unlikely Environmentalists: Congress and the Clean Water Act, 1945–1972*. Lawrence: University Press of Kansas, 2006.

Muskie, Edmund S. *Journeys*. New York: Doubleday, 1972.

Odell, Rice. *Environmental Awakening*. Cambridge, MA: Ballinger, 1980.

Stoddard, Andrew, et al. *Municipal Wastewater Treatment: Evaluating Improvements in National Water Quality*. New York: Wiley, 2002.

COURT CASES

Carabell v. United States Army Corps of Engineers, 547 U.S. 715 (2006).

Environmental Defense et al. v. Duke Energy Corp., 549 U.S. 561 (2007).

Massachusetts v. Environmental Protection Agency, 549 U.S. 497 (2007).

Missouri v. Illinois, 200 U.S. 496 (1906).

Rapanos v. United States, 547 U.S. 715 (2006) (together with Carabell).

Train v. City of New York, 420 U.S. 35 (1975).

Documents and Federal Statutes
"Air pollution—1970. Hearings, Ninety-first Congress, 2nd sess.," on S. 3229, S. 3466 [and] S. 3546, part 2 (March 19, 20, 23, 1970).
Air Quality Act (Clean Air Act of 1967).
Clean Air Act of 1963.
Clean Air Act of 1970.
Clean Air Act Amendments of 1977.
Clean Air Act Amendments of 1990.
Clean Water Act Amendments of 1977.
Clean Water Restoration Act of 1966.
Clean Water Restoration Act of 2009 (proposed).
Comprehensive Environmental Response, Compensation and Liability Act (CERCLA) of 1980 (Superfund Law).
Congressional Record, "Proceedings and Debates of the 92nd Congress," Bill S. 2770, October 4 and 18, 1972.
Constitution of the Commonwealth of Massachusetts.
Federal Water Pollution Control Act of 1948.
Federal Water Pollution Control Act of 1956.
Federal Water Pollution Control Act of 1972 (Clean Water Act).
Federal Water Quality Act of 1965.
Federal Water Quality Act of 1987.
National Air Pollution Control Act.
National Environmental Policy Act.
Ocean Dumping Act of 1972.
Ocean Dumping Ban Act of 1987.
Oil Pollution Act.
Oil Pollution Act Amendments (1966).
Rivers and Harbors Act of 1899.
Safe Drinking Water Act.

Interviews/Recordings
Billings, Leon. Author interview. February 17, 2009.
Environmental Protection Agency scientist/manager (requested anonymity). Author interview. July 19, 2009.
Greenberg, Jon. "Building on the Success of the Clean Water Act." New Hampshire Public Radio, July 23, 2008.
Hunter-Gault, Charlayne, and Jim Lehrer. "Remembering Ed Muskie." *NewsHour*, PBS, March 26, 1996. www.pbs.org/newshour/bb/remember/muskie_3-26.html.
Muskie Oral History Project, Lewiston, ME: Edmund S. Muskie Archives and Special Collections Library, Bates College. Various interviews.
Newman, Randy. "Burn On." *Sail Away*. Rhino/WEA, 1972.
Public Broadcasting Service. "Frederick Jackson Turner." *New Perspectives on the West*. The West Film Project, 2001. www.pbs.org/weta/thewest/people/s_z/turner.htm.
Rancourt, Craig. Author interview. February 9, 2009.

Clean Air and Clean Water Acts

WEBSITES

American Meteorological Society: History of the Clean Air Act
www.ametsoc.org/Sloan/cleanair/index.html

Clean Water Campaign
www.cleanwatercampaign.org

Clean Water Network
www.cleanwaternetwork.org

Dirksen Congressional Center
www.congresslink.org

Edmund S. Muskie Archives & Special Collections
http://abacus.bates.edu/muskie-archives/

Edmund S. Muskie Foundation
www.muskiefoundation.org/

Environmental Defense Fund
www.edf.org

Library of Congress, American Memory section
http://memory.loc.gov/ammem/collections

Muskie School of Public Service
http://muskie.usm.maine.edu

National Archives and Records Administration
www.archives.gov

Natural Resources Defense Council
www.nrdc.org

Poland on the Web
http://info-poland.buffalo.edu/web/history/Polonians/muskie/link.shtml

Rachel Carson Organization
www.RachelCarson.org

Sierra Club Clean Air/Clean Water Sites
www.sierraclub.org/cleanair/ and www.sierraclub.org/cleanwater/

U.S. Congress
www.house.gov (House of Representatives) and www.senate.gov (Senate)

U.S. Environmental Protection Agency
www.epa.gov

Water Pollution Prevention and Control, U.S. Code, Title 33, Chapter 26
www4.law.cornell.edu/uscode/33/ch26.html

All websites accessible as of November 8, 2010.

Index

Page numbers in **boldface** are illustrations.

About the Author

SUSAN DUDLEY GOLD has worked as a reporter for a daily newspaper, managing editor of two statewide business magazines, and freelance writer for several regional publications. She has written more than four dozen books for middle-school and high-school students on a variety of topics, including American history, health issues, law, and space.

Gold has won numerous awards for her work, including most recently the selection of Loving v. Virginia: *Lifting the Ban Against Interracial Marriage*, part of Marshall Cavendish's Supreme Court Milestones series, as one of the Notable Social Studies Trade Books for Young People in 2009. Three other books in that series have received recognition: United States v. Amistad: *Slave Ship Mutiny*, selected as a Carter G. Woodson Honor Book in 2008; and Tinker v. Des Moines: *Free Speech for Students* in 2008 and Roberts v. Jaycees: *Women's Rights* in 2010, both awarded first place in the National Federation of Press Women's communications contest, nonfiction juvenile book category.

Gold has written several titles in the Landmark Legislation series for Marshall Cavendish. She is the author of a number of books on Maine history. She and her husband, John Gold, own and operate a web design and publishing business in Maine. They have one son, Samuel; a granddaughter, Callie; and a grandson, Alexander.